THE
Rise of Chaos
< g e n e s i s >

VOLUME 1

Aeyla Reed

rean_kidd

VANIXIAN
Publishing Studios L.L.C.

The Rise of Chaos: Genesis Volume 1

Illustration by rean_kidd
Character design by mokachaos

The Rise of Chaos: Genesis
By Aeyla Reed
Illustration by rean_kidd
Copyright © 2020 by Aeyla Reed

Visit us at https://theriseofchaos.com || twitter.com/the_riseofchaos

First paperback edition: March 2021

ISBN: 978-1-7362481-0-2

THE of Rise chaos

<genesis>

Aeyla Reed

rean_kidd

PROLOGUE

Impossibly high hewed-stone walls border the city of Axio in its entirety. They stretched even along the southern coast's seaside cliffs. In the center of the city, a tall tower rose into the heavens atop a plateau. From this central spire, partition walls wind through the various districts.

The western most district was home to the Vanixian Republic. They were the surviving denizens of a once mighty empire that spanned the known continent. The Vanixian Empire had fallen some forty years ago, after the *Great Apocalypse*. A name given to an unknown event that caused the spread of demonic creatures, called monsters, across the known world.

The Empire did not have the technological or magickal know-how to defend against the threat of these monsters. After the fall of Tolin, the Empire's largest and strongest port city, the surviving son of the Emperor, Theodin Vanixi, rallied the desolate and panicked human survivors and traveled far north to a coastal peninsula.

They founded a new city and with it; a new government. A Triumvirate, led by three Republics: Vanixian, Maarin, and Renaultian.

Throughout the last decade the three Republic's politics grew increasingly divergent, culminating in the city's physical division.

Since the founding of Axio each Republic has maintained active military forces, called Divisionals. These armies were trained to combat the threats of monsters outside of the city. But tensions were rising between the Republics. Vanixian High Command has given the order that all members stationed in Axio be trained in more conventional methods.

BANG!

The door to my chambers swung open, slamming hard against the stone walls. The sudden disturbance hurled me from my thoughts.

I shot up from my chair in a panic. At the doorway leaned a tall man in an elegant, gold trimmed, plate armored uniform. Strands of dark brown hair clung to his head—though, a single grouping of strands had been dyed a crimson-red. Beads of sweat gleamed down his face.

This was Julius Adaemus, my vice-commander.

I was about to demand he explain the reason for the late night outburst, but I noticed his labored breath.

"Juli—" I started moving towards him, and was interrupted.

"Your father... he's been killed." His words broken through gasps of air.

As Julius spoke, another man pushed past him into the room. An insignia affixed to his collar plate designated him as a military officer, a Knight-Captain.

"The Regent-Lord has been assassinated. Commander Vanixi, you must leave the palace!"

Stunned, I stared blankly at the two men.

What had they just said? My father... is dead?

"We have to..." another gasp of breath, "...to go, Airis." Julius took my arm and pulled me out into the palace halls.

The Knight-Captain shouted out to Julius as we left, "Take her out through the gardens, there should be a carriage waiting."

What in the Aether was happening?

The quietness and seclusion of my bed chambers were a stark difference to the commotion unfolding here.

Guardsmen were frantically running through the narrow corridors of the residential wing. A woman in a Knight's uniform was ushering two men into a side room. Violent shouting echoed down the hallway from behind us, and two guards rounded a corner carrying a large wooden crate marked 'EXPLOSIVES'.

"Move it—out of the way!" The guard in front shouted, strong-arming everyone in his way.

Julius pushed me with his body into a doorway to avoid them. When he started moving again, I pulled back from him.

"What about my sister? And my mother?"

He shook his head.

"Sorry, Airis, I ran straight here." His frantic breathing had caught up a bit. "Isn't your sister away studying?"

I racked my mind. He was right. She should had left this morning to return to her artificer trade-school. I was away at a briefing, but Rias was probably safe. My mother could still be in the palace.

I looked back the way we had come. Her chambers were on the other side of the wing. If I doubled back...

Julius shifted uncomfortably in the hallway in response to a door slamming open.

He reached for my hand. "I'm sure Lady Koharu has been evacuated by the guards. Let's not waste anymore time dawdling."

He was right again. Probably.

I shook my head in an attempt to bring some sense back to it. Being stubborn and searching the palace for my mother was a waste of time.

"I'm not dawdling."

I refused his hand but moved into the hall after him.

We ran through the main hall and down a servant's quarter stairwell to the first floor of the palace. People were running through these halls as well. Their arms full with sacks, boxes, and miscellaneous baubles. We escaped the mayhem through a side entrance and found ourselves alone in the courtyard.

The palace gates were wide open. Flames licked the stone archway of the gatehouse. A number of smaller fires had also been set in the surrounding buildings.

Bodies laid slain on the paved pathway heading out the gate. Some wore the crimson red of the Vanixian Republic, but others wore the green and blue of the Maarin and Renaultian Republics.

This wasn't just some assassination. This was open treason.

Soldiers were fighting in the city streets. The clash of steel rang out as swords crossed in front of us. A group of three heavily armored soldiers were defending against a group of seven. The larger group varied in its composition, two heavy armored warriors were in front with tower shields, two medium armored warriors flanked them, and three lighter clothed casters were in the rear.

The aggressors wore green sashes and clothes. The three retreating soldiers were in red.

"Julius, we have to help!" I dug my heels into the edges of a stone paver and pulled back against Julius.

"We do not have time," his response was spoken harshly, through gritted teeth, "You have to get out of the city before they find you."

"I am not letting these bastards murder our people in the streets!"

"..."

His head shook in disbelief.

"Please, don't get us killed."

He drew his sword and charged towards the spell casters.

I channeled energy through my body, a soft golden glow built around my left hand. The light intensified, and I traced a simple sigil in the air with my finger.

With a closed fist, I aimed my hand at the closest warrior.

"In the light of divinity, be judged. Righteous Fire!"

Upon opening my hand, a dazzling golden flame shot forth closing the distance between us in seconds.

My HOLY BOLT impacted against the leather breastplate, puncturing it, leaving a gaping wound in their side. A cry of pain rang out, and the warrior doubled over.

The group turned to see who had just vaporized the chest of their comrade, and I became the center of attention of the enemy group.

Julius took advantage of the distraction and leapt forward, thrusting his blade into the throat of one of the casters. It sank deep and the man collapsed. Julius pushed the body off his sword with his foot, an arc of arterial blood sprayed from his target's neck as his blade came free.

With a powerful swing, his blade contacted the next caster in line. It cut across their unprotected midsection. They fumbled backwards and flailed on the ground for a moment before ceasing.

"Hwaaaaarrh!"

One of the Vanixian soldiers cried out while charging forward. He wielded a two-handed great sword. It was held low by his right side as he ran into the enemy. A powerful swing struck hard against a tower shield, the impact knocked both the attacker and defender backwards.

The other two Vanixians capitalized on the knockdown effect and charged in to flank the remaining shield user.

Julius' attention turned to the remaining caster in the rear. A glow of blue light had been gathering around their hands, but when the great sword attack impacted the loud bang must have interrupted their concentration. A jolt of energy spread through her arms and she yelped in shock. She turned heel and fled—but didn't make it far.

A fiery ball crashed down from the direction of the gatehouse. It impacted the fleeing caster, and charred chunks of flesh and bone spattered against the surrounding walls and street.

In the same instant, a volley of arrows penetrated through the armor of the three remaining Maarin soldiers.

I spun around to see who our reinforcements were, expecting a few straggling Divisionals—instead, a sea of crimson met my gaze. In formation, a mass of hundreds marched down the street. They were led by a small woman with wild cherry-red hair, dressed in an ornately embroidered uniform. Golden trim traced the edges of a light steel breastplate, affixed to which was a Commander's insignia. I recognized her.

This was Hailey Brooks, Commander of the Third Division.

The three soldiers Julius and I had jumped in to save approached her, but an officer blocked them, pointing to the rest of the formation. They saluted and fell in towards the back. Hailey glanced over at my companion. Her eyes narrowed.

"Julius?"

"Commander Brooks." He responded nonchalantly.

Her eyes widened. Likely from the implication that if High-Protector Julius Adaemus was here, then so too would Commander Airis Vanixi. Her calm and leader-like composure fled, her eyes frantically scanned the streets for me. I gave a second of thought to trying to garner her attention with a wave, but it didn't matter. Before I could even raise my arm, she had spotted me.

"Airis!" She ran towards me and stopped short within an arm's reach.

Hailey and I had attended Axio's military academy for nobles youths together, the Vanixian Academy for Divisional Officers, or 'VxA' for short. Though it had been a few years since I had seen her last. She looked the same, and was even emitting the same youthful energy as back then.

"Oh, heya, Hails. It's... uh, been awhile." I chuckled.

My arm was bent with a hand resting above my shoulder. I was trying my best not to be awkward. Even in normal circumstances, my interpersonal skills weren't up to kit, let alone in the middle of a battle.

She remained unfazed by my stumbling greeting.

"I'm so glad you're safe! I heard about everything from a runner to our garrison..." her words trailed off and she shook her head, "I mobilized my Division straight to the palace, but you had already left. We gathered up anyone we could and were heading to the main gate—"

Julius approached and interrupted her, "We need to keep moving. You're not safe here."

Hailey nodded in agreement.

"He's right, come with us. Let's get you to safety."

"A large group like this will slow us down."

"Yeah maybe! But a large group will also keep you from being overwhelmed if another patrol spots you!"

"We weren't spotted! We were assisting those other soldiers!"

The two of them bickered for a few moments. Ultimately, it didn't matter. Fate had already made my decision for me.

During the time they had been arguing, I had pulled a small golden coin from my pocket.

In the glow of the distant flames, the polished faces flickered as it tumbled through the air. The coin landed on the back of my palm.

Heads, I would escape the city. Just Julius and I.

Tails, I'd stay and do what I could to lead my people to safety.

I lifted my palm slowly to reveal Fate's decision. A crimson-red painted engraving of a Phoenix, its feathered wings spread wide, stared up at me...

Tails.

ONE

FLAMES ILLUMINATED THE NIGHT SKY ABOVE
Axio. Fire engulfed the city around me. Thick clouds of
smoke clung to the city walls.

The smell of charred flesh stung my nose.

Soaring towers of stone crumbled under pressure as
their roofs caved in.

The sounds of steel clashing and the crackle of magick
rang in my ears...

"Heads."

A dry voice hurtled me from my thoughts.

I was no longer in the streets of Axio. Rather, I was in
a room above a tavern in the outskirts of patrolled
territory, called the Commonlands. More precisely, I was
slumped over in the sill of a small window, lost in
thought, as the sun drifted towards the horizon. It had
been quiet in the room for hours while I stared out past
the hills and trees. The last rays of light glinted in the
distance.

I turned around to respond to my companion, but all
I could see was a darkened room.

Celestials above, it's pitch black in here!

I allowed my eyes to adjust enough to avoid fumbling
around entirely, and found the table that was centered in
the room.

I sparked a piece of flint against a steel striker over a pair of candles and shadows danced around the room in the soft glow.

"Aaah, that's better." I sighed, "Julius, you haven't said a word to me all day and the first thing you want to do is bet on a coin toss?"

I shook my head.

"You can't possibly know that it's heads anyway."

"It's always heads."

Julius sat down at the table and looked at me expectantly. I grabbed my pack and dug out a small map and laid it out across the table, gently moving the candles to avoid spilling any wax. Julius kicked out the chair opposite of him, and I sat down.

"Well, it wasn't heads last time."

"Last time..." His turn to sigh, "Airis, the last time you flung that coin in the air, the day ended with Republic soldiers chasing us through the streets of Axio. So it doesn't count."

"Yeah, I suppose. Oh!-there was that time at the bakery—and the time at the docks! It's been tails a bunch of times ya' know."

Arms crossed, he leaned back in his chair, "It's definitely heads this time." The candlelight flickered and his face faded into the shadows on the wall. I sat in silence for awhile, looking over the map.

"I haven't even decided if I'm flipping the coin this time."

He lunged forward and pointed a finger at my face, "We both know that's a load of shit. I've watched you rolling that coin through your fingers for the last hour."

I smacked his hand away from my face and gave him a soured look.

"Paaffh!" he let out a huff and sat back in the shadows, "I know you're flipping the coin, and you know it too. I called heads."

I let the coin slide back into my palm. He was right.

The idea of letting a coin toss make a decision was the embodiment of Fate to me.

Would fate side with my second-in-command or myself?

With that thought, I sent the coin spiraling into the air with a flick of my thumb. Candlelight sparkled off the polished faces.

A moment later and the flash of gold landed on the back of my hand, quickly covered from view by my other hand.

Slowly I lifted my palm up to peek at the outcome. On my hand sat the ornate engraving of a Phoenix. My eyes drifted from the coin to Julius.

His head hung down, letting out a sigh of defeat.

"Where are we going?"

He knew it wasn't heads.

"..."

I have got to work on my bluffing skills.

I hovered over the crudely drawn map. Tapping the coin against the table in my right hand, I fidgeted with the creases of the parchment with my left. My eyes darted across the rivers and mountains spanning the southern coast of Axio's domain. I had decided our next move yesterday, but I hadn't quite built up the confidence to tell Julius my plan.

"So... where in the Aether are we going?" He asked again, agitation in his voice.

"Tolin."

"Hah! Suicide."

"And why is it suicide?"

"There is nothing in Tolin. Maybe rebels, monsters— Oh, and bandits hiding in the mountains! This tavern is practically as far south as the Republic's guards patrol."

"We are rebels, Julius."

"I'm not a rebel."

"We were tried, and convicted."

"Bah! Guilty of..." he trailed off, "...uh, Celestials above, how did that condescending magistrate put it?"

"I believe his words were," I cleared my throat, and with a pompous accent continued, "Charged with conspiracy to commit treason against the Triumvirate Republics and their citizens."

"Yeah, that was it. Sounds just like him. Anyway, being guilty of 'treason' doesn't make us rebels. It makes us fugitives."

Hard to argue with that logic. The subtle difference didn't change the situation we were in.

Julius stood and walked over to the window. The rhythmic thumping of him tapping his thumb against the sill interrupted the brief silence. He wasn't one to fidget idly with his hands.

Was he nervous?

Celestials above, I knew I was... I wanted to break the tension but didn't know what the right thing was to say.

"Well, it's not suicide if we had an army with us."

"And what army are we? Some noblewoman and her bodyguard?"

"I'm more than some noblewoman. And you're more than just a bodyguard—though you do make a good one." I snickered. "And for 'what army', the Fourth Division has a supply regiment stationed at a checkpoint five miles south of us, before the mountain pass."

Without any orders coming from Axio, that convoy should still be posted at the checkpoint. I was betting on them still being there.

"..."

Julius didn't have a snarky response for that. He continued staring out the window, likely mulling over the idea of a rendezvous with the scattered Divisional Army. Ten minutes had passed before he finally asked another question.

"Why Tolin?"

I took a moment to think over a proper response to his question. It wasn't much anymore, but many years ago Tolin was one of the most profitable trading ports in the Empire.

It was a fortress city built on a peninsula along the coast of the Southern Plains. Positioned so that the only way to get to it from Axio was either by sea, or through a precarious mountain pass.

"Airis," Julius snapped me from my thoughts once again. He was looking at me with a frown. "Hey! What is in Tolin?"

"Well, nothing I suppose. But, the plan is anyway, I'm going to take the regiment stationed at the pass and we'll march our way to Tolin, storm the city gates, and reclaim the city as our own."

I stood there in a heroic pose. My left hand rested on the back of the chair, my right was high in the air holding an invisible sword. A big smile stretched across my face.

"Oh, okay. That's all then. We take command of an outpost of divisionals and march them through some dangerous mountains. Then storm a city filled with horrors even the Celestials themselves don't want to deal with. All to lay claim to the largest port the Empire ever created?"

Julius was trying to hide the biggest smile I've seen on his face in days.

"It's the craziest plan I've ever heard. When are we leaving?"

My focus was back to the map. I traced my fingers across a river-way that defined the border of the Commonlands to the Southern Plains. I needed to remember where the route south branched out. I wanted to spend the night planning out our route and inspecting our gear. This tavern would be the last hospitable stop for the next few days. Without looking up I responded to him.

"Early morning. Tomorrow."

"Sounds like a plan then. Good, because this place was starting to feel a little too... comfortable."

His more than dramatic pause before, and emphasis on, the word 'comfortable' garnered my attention. I stopped obsessing over my map.

This was his way of insinuating something.

"Uh-huh, we've only been here two days—my back is already starting to act up. How are you 'too comfortable'?"

He sat in silence, knowing that I had caught him in the act.

"The innkeeper is too… nice. And… uh, the servers at the bar keep trying to get me drunk."

I stared at him dumbfounded. He got me. I fell right into his trap. By the Celestials above, there was no way I could breeze past that statement.

"The innkeeper is too nice!? And that is what bar staff are supposed to do." I shook my head and sighed. I pointed at him, "And, that doesn't answer my question. I know what you're doing. Stop deflecting."

He crossed his arms, "I wasn't going to say anything but—the idea of staying in the same place for any longer seemed like poor judgment. You've been holed up in this room the entire time we've been here!"

"Ohhhh, I was getting too comfortable you meant."

"You didn't seem like you had a plan to leave any time soon, is all."

I was enjoying the time to rest.

I wasn't about to lie to myself or Julius and pretend otherwise. We had been traveling at breakneck speed for over a week straight. But I was also planning. I didn't have time to leave the room.

That, and I didn't want to deal with any nosey people.

"Well, we're leaving tomorrow. So, no need to worry."

Julius turned back to stare out the window. The game was over. I wasn't sure if I won or not, but it mattered little in the grand scheme of his torments.

I leaned back in my chair and traced over a runic symbol tattooed on my left wrist. Aetheric mists formed in front of me and the rune illuminated. The rune projected a light unto the mist, creating a visual interface which allowed me to review core details.

I manipulated the interface to show a breakdown of my physical and mental attributes, and a list of equipment and items in my possession.

ATTRIBUTES		CLASS SPECIALIZATION: Paladin	
STRENGTH	24	VITALITY	18
TOUGHNESS	5	ENDURANCE	5
FORTITUDE	23	STAMINA	17
COURAGE	44	RESOLVE	34
AGILITY	5	DEXTERITY	26
SWIFTNESS	5 -1	CLEVERNESS	32
PERCEPTION	5	FINESSE	5
REFLEX	5	INGENUITY	41
AETHER	19		
INTELLIGENCE	33 +5		
WISDOM	21		
SANITY	5		

GRIMOIRE   MAGICKAL SPECIALIZATION: Divine Light

SPELL	SCHOOL	CLASS	DESCRIPTION
HEAL (MAJOR)	Holy	Action	Heals a major wound. Requires touch range
HEAL (MINOR)	Holy	Action	Heals a minor wound. Requires touch range
AURA OF LIGHT	Holy	Combat	Increases the effectiveness of healing magicks.
BRILLIANCE (MINOR)	Arcane	Action	Increases the power of spells and their chance to critical cast.
HOLY BOLT	Holy	Action	Inflicts minor damage. Inflicts moderate damage to Undead and Demons.
OVERSIGHT	Arcane	Passive	Allows the caster to visualize party members and targets battle statistics.

EQUIPMENT

ITEM	ATTRIBUTES	DESCRIPTION
WORN LEATHER CHEST-PIECE	+12 Armor -1 Swiftness	A chest-guard with shoulder protectors made of stiff leather.
YEW STAFF	10-12 Damage +5 Intelligence	A grooved wooden staff, with a small crystal for focusing spells
RUGGED LEATHER BOOTS	+5 Armor	A sturdy pair of leather boots.
LINEN HAND-WRAPS	+1 Armor	Strips of linen from a sheet torn and fastened into hand wraps.
WORN DENIM TROUSERS	+2 Armor	Cotton-woven pants. Fashionable and practical.
LINEN BLOUSE	-	A simple linen blouse.
STEEL DAGGER	25-36 Damage	A thick steel bladed dagger with a leather grip.
SIMPLE LEATHER BELT	-	A thin leather belt with a worn bronze buckle.
CELESTIAL SYMBOL	Relic	A holy symbol depicting an angelic image of the Celestial, Capricorn.
VANIXIAN COIN	Relic	A well-worn coin engraved with a Phoenix and the Vanixian Imperial Coat-of-Arms.

With a double-tap of the runic symbol with my finger the projection faded and the mists dissipated.

Looking up, I glanced over to where Julius had been, but he had moved. He was now tipped back in a chair against the wall next to the window. His face was obscured by his own rune's mist projection.

An exasperated sigh overcame me.

I needed to give some serious thought about what we're going to do once we've reached the outpost. I should be able to take command well enough.

Julius' face may not be recognized as easily, but I was the daughter of the Regent Lord—and a decorated Commander to boot! Any officer at that post should be able to vouch for us.

The trouble was getting to that officer. That is going to be the hard part. It was likely that they've received news of the coup in Axio. Maybe even some of the survivors made it there already.

It would be our luck that some nerve racked Initiate keeping watch sees us and decides asking questions aren't on the table. We're probably going to have a really bad time.

"Ugh!" I cried out to nobody in particular.

Urrrggrll.

My stomach growled, shattering my thoughts of frustration. By the Celestials, I haven't eaten almost all day. I got up to head out of our room, but stopped and looked over at Julius. He was passed out in his chair, mist projection still active.

That was fast. Well, I don't want to wake him up. I'll grab something simple from the kitchen on my way back for him.

I left the room and headed down the hall to the staircase, stopping to listen before heading down. All quiet. It must be close to midnight. There would hopefully be nobody down in the tavern and I could get some food in peace.

I walked down the stairs. My hand trailed across the banisters, making a soft 'thump, thump, thump' as I descended.

As I rounded a corner into the hall, a short haired woman emerged from a doorway. She was carrying a platter piled with dirty dishes and glassware.

Her sudden appearance surprised me. My heart skipped and I clutched my chest as I jumped backwards out of her way.

Her head whipped to me and her eyes flashed with surprise.

"Oh—Miss, you startled me!" The soft clank of glass hitting against glass rang down the halls as she steadied herself. "If you're looking for the tavern it is just through here," she indicated behind her with a nod, "I'll be back in a minute to get you settled in. Feel free to sit anywhere!"

"U-Uhm... thank you." I let her pass by and headed into the tavern.

The main bar hall of the tavern was spacious and open, with exposed rafters. The bartop was positioned near the center of the room. A short flight of stairs to the right of the bar led up to a single large table. Four smaller tables were lined along the wall from there to the end of the room.

Behind the bar was a tall, slender man. Golden curls cascaded down his narrow face. Long, sharp ears broke through the curls.

He's an elf!

There were very few elves in Axio, and even fewer in the small remote towns in the outskirts of the Commonlands. Seeing an elf here was a rare sight.

Next to him along the bar top slept a curled up cat with striking brown and black markings.

In the middle of the room was a somber group that looked like they were fairly well armed, maybe mercenaries. They had two tables pushed together and we're drinking quietly. I made a mental note to avoid them at all costs. And along the back wall, at one of the smaller tables, was a cowled figure, picking at a plate of food.

I took a seat on a stool at the bar next to the cat. Its ears perked up as I took my seat. One eye slowly crept open to see who had caused the disturbance. The expression wasn't quite one of annoyance... maybe apathy would be the best description.

The bartender looked over to me with a glass in his hands.

"That's Meko, he's good company. I'll let you in on a secret, if you want to get on his good side. Scratch his ears a bit. He loves it." He shook the glass and gave me a 'what will you have' look.

"Ease me in, barkeep. Uh... nothing too strong, I haven't eaten all day."

He thought for a moment and filled the glass from a large keg on the back wall.

"Here, give this one a try."

The glass was warm. I thought about declining the drink. But I couldn't be so picky this far out from Axio. There wouldn't be any ice chilled glasses and cold brews this far from civilization.

He gave me a simple wave as he stepped away, "I'm Nyle, by the way. Just holler if you need anything else. Amelia should be back any minute and can take your food order."

"Thanks, Nyle."

I sipped the drink and was surprised that even though it was warm, it was incredible. The flavor, mainly a sweet fruity one, had a sharp tartness to it. Blackberries and apples.

"Delicious." I let out a content sigh.

Meko, now eyes fully open, stared at me expectantly. I gave his ears a little scratch. He purred and leaned his head into my hand.

"Good kitty."

The tavern door opened, and in bounced the woman from the hall. She glanced over at the mercenary table but came straight to me.

"Hello again! I'm Amelia. My shift just started so you'll be stuck with me all night!" She said with a laugh.

Whoa. That's a lot of energy for midnight, lady.

She continued, "Are you hungry? I can get something put together for you from the kitchen." She glanced down to my drink and before I even had a chance to answer, "Oh! I know just the thing to go with that, I'll be right back."

She took off towards the kitchen.

I don't even know what I want... So I guess this is fine?

I continued scratching Meko absentmindedly and turned my attention to the mercenary-like group. It was odd for a party this big to be this far from the city. Anyone out here either had a disdain for people, or they had some sort of agenda.

I hope they weren't here for Julius and I.

Taking an opportunity to eavesdrop on their conversation, I sipped at my sweet and tart drink and tried to focus on what they were saying. I could only make out partial sentences.

"...Big group... Divisionals..."

"...Red uniforms... some little woman leading them..."

"...Think they might hire us?"

"...Doubtful they... with people like us..."

Red uniformed Divisionals!?

It sounded like more of us did make it out of Axio. I pondered at who they were referring to leading them. If it was who I thought it was, this whole 'suicide mission' wouldn't actually be suicide.

The conversation trailed off and the words became less interesting. They were likely members of Axio's Adventurer's Guild and were out here looking for work. I relaxed and focused back to something much more important...

I doubled my efforts scratching Meko, to the reward of deep content purring.

Amelia returned with a plate, steam billowed up. Glistening brisket covered in sauce was laid between two braided wheat buns. Cheese dripped down the edges, mixing around the sandwich in a pool of juice. She placed the plate down in front of me and waved her arms, presenting me with my glorious feast.

"Your dinner, miss. I hope you like it."

"This looks and smells amazing!"

I took a bite and my taste buds exploded as the sandwich practically melted in my mouth.

"Celestials above, this is the best thing I've had since—in a while." I caught myself.

"Glad you like it, miss... what was your name? I don't think I caught it earlier"

I froze in a slight panic, but only for a moment. Nobody out here is going to be big into Axio city politics. And even then, unless they have a military background they wouldn't know who I am... Nonetheless I needed to be careful.

"O-Oh. Uhm..." I stammered, "My name's Airis."

Great job. Super inconspicuous. You're doing wonderful at being careful, Airis. That awkward pause wasn't long at all.

Amelia squinted at me. A seriousness took form on her face and she leaned in close. In a hushed voice that could barely be considered a whisper, she spoke into my ear.

"Like, the Airis? Airis Vanixi?"

I was absolutely wrong. You're doing terrible at being careful, Airis. Time to panic!

My nerves plummeted. The hairs on the back of my neck raised as a natural fight-or-flight emotion rushed through my body.

What the heck does she mean by 'the Airis'? Like I'm some sort of wanted criminal out here!

I could run upstairs and force Julius awake. We'd flee in the middle of the night like the fugitives we were. Or I could try to keep calm and hope for the best—No, there was no way I could play it off and pretend that I wasn't the person she insinuated.

She connected my name to my family's house instantly. There was no way she doesn't know who I am.

Amelia must have seen the panic spread across my face like wildfire because her reaction was quick. In the time I fumbled to come up with a plan of escape she gripped my forearms and started reassuring me,

"No-no-no it's okay!" She pulled a stool out beside me, "Your secret is safe with me."

More hushed words. But there was a sincerity in her voice that pulled at me to trust her.

She continued in a whisper, "It was about six days ago. A giant army came through here and set up camp on the village border. A small group came in here for rooms, probably officers or other fancy titles. The one in charge was a joyful lady, full of smiles and laughs. She was on the shorter side and I think she said her name was Hailey. They had a few drinks here, naturally I asked them what they were doing out here..." she sighed deeply.

My nerves had settled during her brief pause and I took another bite of my sandwich. The juicy meat had soaked the bread and some sauce dripped down the corner of my mouth. I grasped around frantically for a napkin but there was no hope for me. Thankfully, Amelia handed me a cloth from her waist and I wiped my messiness away.

With my dramatic antics resolved, Amelia continued on, "They told me about the coup in Axio. That the Renault and Maarin forces had attacked and the Vanixian government was in shambles."

She gave me a soft look accompanied with a smile. Her voice no longer hushed, she kept on, "They said that there was a commander, named Airis Vanixi, who gave the order for the rest of them to retreat. Is that true? That you stayed behind to give people a chance to escape?"

I had to take a moment to absorb the whole story. While it was true that I had stayed behind after giving orders to flee the city. It wasn't just me. A small group of us, including Julius, stayed behind. Though it wasn't nearly as heroic as Amelia's story made it out to be. It wasn't like we were making some grand last stand, screaming into the night that we'd never surrender. Instead we gave up with no resistance. I knew that if they had captured me, interest in those retreating would vanish.

Hailey Brooks, Commander of the Third Divisionals. She made it out of Axio, and managed to get a 'giant army' this far south. As far as bad plans go, ours seemed to work out.

Lost in thought, my glance drifted over to Amelia, who was looking at me expectantly. I nodded my head, "Yeah, it was. But, it wasn't just me that stayed behind. I was captured—but escaped during a second attack. The Maarin Republic launched an attack on the Renaultians that same night..."

Amelia turned to the bar and called out, "Hey Nyle, can we get a few more of these *Tartapple* ciders?"

A silent nod and a moment later two new glasses of the sweet and tart drink I had been served earlier were set down in front of us.

For the next hour Amelia told me everything she had heard from Axio. Information from other refugees or passing travelers.

Eventually my eyes started to become heavy. Amelia must have been able to tell that I was tired. She stood from her place at the bar and started to clear the glassware.

"I'll let you get some sleep. I should probably clean up these other tables."

Meko had curled up in my lap. I gave him a final scratch and he leapt up to his perch on the counter.

I tried to stifle a yawn but failed and was overtaken with intense exhaustion, "I do need to get to bed. I've got an early morning coming. Hey, could you grab me something simple from the kitchen? I have a friend upstairs who hasn't eaten either, but I didn't want to wake him."

"Of course!" She ran back to the kitchen and in a flash was back with a cloth wrapped bundle. "Stop by in the morning and you can settle up your bill."

I opened the door to my room slowly to avoid making any noise. Julius was sound asleep in the chair where I left him. The bundle from Amelia found a home on the table. And I found a home on the edge of my bed.

I tied my hair up with a strip of linen, and laid my head down on a soft feathered pillow. I fidgeted my feet around and managed to kick both of my boots off. I glanced over at Julius once more, to confirm he was sleeping, and peeled off my shirt and pants. I wrapped myself in the sheets of the bed and let my mind drift into the aether...

TWO

I WOKE UP ON COLD, HARD GROUND.

Sharp pains and aches shot through my side as I rolled over. I was no longer in the comforts of a warm bed, instead I was in the middle of a prison cell.

I'm confident I went to sleep in a bed, how did I get here?

The cell was small. Maybe about twelve feet on each side and squared off. It was barely lit and lined with cold stone slabs. There was an opening above me. Far above me.

I laid there for a while studying it. It had to be twenty or thirty feet. The perspective from the floor made it hard to judge.

It was possible that I could climb up and escape. But before I had a chance to formulate a daring escape plan, a bright light appeared in the opening. It was blinding and I raised my arm up to shield my eyes.

But this was not my arm. It was meatier than mine... and hairy. The wrist and palm were wrapped in blood-stained bandages. Large bony fingers protruded from the soaked wraps.

This isn't right... What is happening?

A door slammed loudly down the hallway followed by shouts that echoed against the stone. The voices became clearer as their source approached closer to the cell.

"Why can't we just kill the girl?"

"Because Fontaine told the Capt' to keep 'er alive, at least until tomorrow."

"Hangings are too boring. I don't just want to watch her squirm, I want to make her squirm.."

"Celestials above, you're a psychopath."

"Screw you. Anyways, Capt' didn't say we couldn't rough 'em up a bit. And I'm gonna make this one cry for his mum."

The men stopped in front of my cell and I lifted my head to look at them, but their faces were blurry—as if obscured by a fog. There were three men in total, and the one in the center spoke first.

"Get up, dirt-bag."

He had a long blue uniform coat that dipped down past his knees. A Renaultian insignia on his coat was displayed prominently, but I couldn't quite make out the rank. It was also distorted by a fog. The other two men had much simpler uniform jackets on but the same fog hung around their ranks. All three of them towered over me at over six feet. They were too tall to just be regular Renaultian Divisionals. They were probably legionnaires from one of the nomadic tribes.

The man who spoke first kicked the cell. Metal scraped against stone. A sharp echo rang down the hall. In an angry tone he sneered at me.

"Hey! Dirt-bag, I said get up."

I stood up and looked... down at him—*Looked down? I wouldn't look down at anyone over six feet tall.*

This had to be some sort of dream. But I wasn't in my body. A sort of nightmare then. It felt so real.

Words came from my mouth, but they weren't my words. A hoarse voice. "I don't care about what you have to say, you bluecoat ass."

I know that voice. It's Julius' voice. Is this a memory?

There was always a distinct possibility that I was having a stroke.

The man spit on me—Well, not me...

On Julius.

Completely out of my own control, my arms reached through the bars and grabbed his throat with one hand and his coattails with the other. His very surprised face was pulled towards the bars and slammed against the steel. My hands let go just as his face made contact.

Celestials above!

The man stumbled back and yelled out in pain. Julius' voice growled out of my mouth, "You don't get to talk about her." The three men did not appreciate his lesson in social politics. The door to the cell was opened. They stepped in and more shouting was heard from down the hall.

Great, more people are coming to see the fun. I readied myself for a fight that never came. A loud explosion deafened me. The back wall of the cell blew out and knocked me off my feet...

"Hey! Airis, hey! Wake up!"

I awoke to Julius, who was kneeling down next to my bed, poking my forehead with his finger. My body was damp with sweat. It had soaked through the sheets, causing them to stick to me as I tried to sit up. He gave me a discerning look, "Do you want to talk about whatever weird panic attack you just had or—"

"No."

I pushed him away and tried to unstick myself from the bed. I glared at him and he turned around. I threw my shirt over my head and scrambled into the pair of pants. The faint glow of light breaking through the window. "Celestials above, what time is it?"

"Just before dawn." His curt reply was paired with his hand grabbing something from the table. That something was then thrown straight at my face. A direct hit, and a muffin fell onto my lap. "You good?"

"Yeah. Yeah I'm fine. Exhausted is all."

I bit into my face-muffin. There were big chunks of Hallonut throughout the whole thing. It was absolutely disgusting. I took another bite and noticed my wrist was glowing with a pulsing light. I tapped the rune embed there and mists displayed a notification,

» YOU HAVE EXPERIENCED A PSYCHOMETRIC EPISODE

Uhm. What in the Aether is that supposed to mean?

I shook my head and tapped again to mute the notification. We needed to get ready before the sun had risen completely. I could deal with that psycho-whatever thing later. Nightmares and panic attacks were becoming a common occurrence for me since we left Axio. But not quite as unusual as this.

Leather armor padding pressed hard against my chest as I fit the straps and buckles of my chestguard into place. Pulling a dagger from my pack, I gently trimmed a few stray threads from my trousers. The dagger was then sheathed in a makeshift scabbard on my right leg. After a brief search I found my boots and laced them tightly. My equipment was a mismatch sort of anything we could get our hands on for cheap. The escape from Axio left me with nothing but a ragged jumpsuit. I mourned the loss of my tailored and fitted uniform.

Julius' equipment was a different story. Somehow he had managed to make it out of Axio with a fair amount of his own gear. I was only slightly jealous. That's what I convinced myself of anyway.

Julius was facing a mirror making adjustments to his uniform.

The officer's standard issue was a soft-white, sleeved, knee-length coat that curved back into a tail. The masculine styled version was straight-cut, whereas the feminine style was looser and had a more ruffled look.

Depending on the individual the coats ranged from simplistic to ornately adorned.

Some uppercore officers, like Julius and myself, had golden embroidery and red accented sashes, buckles, and leather straps. In addition to the coat, the uniform included matching steel greaves, bracers, breastplate, and pauldrons.

Julius' uniform was one of the more ornately decorated versions. Golden trim accented the steel plates of his protective armor. A crimson red sash hung down his left side below his scabbard. He fidgeted with his insignia until it fit perfectly on his collar. I was watching his attempts to look presentable when he turned to me and raised an eyebrow.

"How do I look?"

Julius was handsome by any standard. His face radiated that of both a careless youth and a battle hardened veteran. A mop of dark brown hair hung around his face, though it was broken by a forelock dyed a vibrant red, the same red as my own hair. It was something he started doing when he came on as my vice-commander. I never truly understood why he did it, but I also didn't mind. It's not like it caused any issues— actually a few of the other junior officers also dyed their hair a similar way, and it became a trend in the First Division.

I playfully looked him over in a mock inspection, pausing every so often to let out a 'hmm' and an 'aaah'. He looked just fine. There wasn't anyone we needed to impress anyway so I wasn't sure why he even cared. I made a few tweaks on his insignias and dusted off his shoulder in an obvious way. Finally I stood back and shrugged.

Julius grinned and said jokingly, "Do I pass muster?"

I shrugged again, "Ahh, your boots could use some polish."

He laughed, but glanced down with a sour look at his boots. Likely contemplating if he could even find boot polish out here in the Commonlands.

He shook his head and pointed down to his breastplate that was resting against a chair nearby. "Would you be a dear and help me put on this deathcage?"

"Why, Protector Julius, I am not your squire." I said wryly.

"That's High-Protector to you, Commander Airis." A grin formed on his face. "Or is it Initiate Airis? Without your uniform I just can't tell."

"Oh, go screw yourself." I said, laughing back at him. "Secondly, It's probably High-Commander Airis now, or don't you remember that my father—" My eyes welled with tears and I turned away.

Ahhh, by the Aether get your shit together Airis.

"Celestials above... Airis, I was just teasing. I didn't mean anything by it." He took a step back and held up his hands in apology.

"Hey, it's fine. That was my fault, I just got myself worked up. It's okay."

I twirled my finger for him to turn around. He held the front plates in place while I pulled the red leather straps through fittings on the rear plate and locked him into his 'deathcage'. On both the front and rear plates were fittings near the shoulders. These were for metal pauldrons that almost every sword wielder would wear. Julius, however, had left them behind when fleeing Axio and was missing both of these pauldrons.

Staring at the dead space above his shoulders, I glanced at the mirror and our eyes met.

"Quit looking at me with those depressing eyes, lets go get something real to eat downstairs." He joked, easing the tension.

I slapped the back of his head, pushing him into the mirror for good measure. I needed something more than muffin. I wanted a whole slab of bacon if I was going to be honest.

"Yeah, let's head down."

I finished packing away our belongings and we headed downstairs to the tavern. Julius took a table in the far back corner that gave us a vantage of the entire room. Amelia saw us from the bar and waved. A moment later she was bouncing over to our table with a pitcher full of water.

"Well, good morning you two! Look at that sharp looking uniform Julius! Quite fetching if I'm to be honest" She turned to me and gave me an exaggerated wink.

I had no clue what it meant.

This woman was entirely too happy after being awake all night. It made me tired to see her so wide awake.

She stood there beaming with energy and just continued on, "What can I get started for you? Jesse just brought up some fresh eggs if you wanted something breakfast-y!"

"Good morning Amy," Julius spoke up first, "I'll have whatever today's meat is, the largest portion of bacon you're allowed to bring me, some hashed potatoes, some oranges, a great big pint of cider... oh and a few of those eggs."

"You got it, love. And for you, miss Airis?"

By the Celestials, that's a lot of food.

Julius was obviously hungry. I wasn't in the same gluttonous spirit as he was and opted for a more simple breakfast.

"I'll take a slightly bigger portion of bacon than the hog over there," I nodded at Julius, "and a pint of cider as well."

Amelia gave us a thumbs up. But before leaving she placed a hand on Julius' shoulder and leaned in. She whispered something in his ear that caused his eyes to widen just a small amount. Then she winked at me and trotted back to the kitchen.

"Sooo..." I started.

"Shut. up."

"What was that all about?"

"That, was her telling me that I had 'lost my chance' because—and I quote, 'A lovely red haired, violet eyed beauty stole my heart away last night'." He gave me an inquisitive look, "So, maybe I should be asking you, miss Airis?"

I exploded in a giggle fit. I couldn't help but laugh uncontrollably at the thought. That Julius, the noble looking knight-in-shining-armor, was just a little peeved that a pretty girl told him she preferred me over him. I let out a long sigh and brought myself back to reality.

My cheeks were still flush but I was able to form coherent words now, "Aaaah. She's too cute. We just had a few drinks last night after you went to bed, that's all."

He sat there pouting. "Uh huh. Nothing else happened?"

"Wouldn't you like to know?"

Julius kept pouting for another minute but dropped his act when Amelia swung by with two large glasses of cider. Tartapple. Delicious! Julius and I shared a cheer and raised our glasses together.

"So, I have some good news. Turns out Commander Brooks passed through here a few days ago—With a large number of Divisionals in tow."

"Your army made manifest."

"She and I went to war-college together, ya' know. If we can find them we'll be in a great position."

I smiled. Well, it was more of a shit-eating grin than a smile. "The Celestials rain blessings down upon me."

"Do they now?" Julius quipped in a snarky tone. "If that was so, don't you think we'd be in Axio, having our breakfast instead of this tavern?"

"Perhaps, the Celestials just work in mysterious ways." I shifted uncomfortably in my seat. I meant it as a joke, but Julius was right. I was certain the Celestials did not rain down any blessings on me. "But how then would the bards know to sing of my greatness and valorous deeds?" I threw a snarky quip back at him and flashed a wicked grin.

"Hah! Greatness indeed. A great big head perhaps?" Julius took a sip of cider and grinned back at me.

"Oh come now, Julius. Perhaps they will sing of your greatness as well." I drummed out a simple melody with my fingers tapping against the table, and sang a short tune. The chorus of which involved a number of gruesome things that happened to 'Sir Julius'. On the second round of the chorus I was cut off—

"By the Aether, Airis! What in the underworld was that!?" he shot daggers with his eyes, a soured look on his face. "Woman, you are not a bard"

And that is what he gets for being a dick earlier. I gave him a big smile. He relaxed after another minute and let out a chuckle.

"Where did you even come up with such terrible lyrics?"

"Well, there was this awful minstrel in Axio that followed one of the noblemen around. Robin, I believe his name was."

"Well I hope that noble fired that minstrel. That was truly terrible. Never sing that again."

I raised my hands in defense, "Like you said, I am no bard."

We were interrupted by the arrival of two large platters of food. Though one was significantly larger than the other. Julius' eyes got wide when he was presented with his feast. My plate had a small bowl filled with red berries. I looked at Amelia questioningly and was met with a look that I could only describe as 'motherly'.

"I know you only asked for bacon," she said pointing at the bowl, "but you really should keep your breakfast balanced with some fruit. It helps keep your head clear." She gave me a big smile and walked away before I could protest.

Julius gave me a stupid look while nodding his head. He pointed to his bowl of oranges and with his mouth already full of food he mumbled, "It's true."

Julius continued to shovel loads of food into his gaping maw. Alchemists would likely one day study the phenomena that was his ability to consume his body weight in food in a single sitting. I picked at my berries and bacon slowly, savoring each bite. It was doubtful we'd have food like this for a while.

Nyle greeted me with a scrawled out breakdown of our charges when I went to clear out tab. The charges were actually reasonable considering how far from the city we were. Totaling sixty-five silver coins in all, I gave Nyle a gold coin from my pack, "That should cover us, don't worry about making change. Please split it with Amelia."

As we were leaving the tavern Amelia spotted us and waved goodbye. Julius and I headed to the stables. I flipped my coin, calling tails for the mare. She didn't buck as often as the stallion. Julius swore at the sky, calling out every Celestial in a heathenish display of sacrilege.

The sun rose quickly.

Julius was riding ahead of me, leading by about two or three lengths. We passed empty clearing in the trees one after another. After an hour the boring ride took a twist on the exciting side. A fog started to roll into the forest. Julius stopped his horse and looked back at me.

"This fog doesn't feel natural, Airis."

I could feel a jolting tingle on my skin, Aethermist. The same condensate appearing in the runic magick I used to view interfaces, Aethermist would form in large amounts when non-elemental magick was performed.

I dropped from my horse and quickly pulled my staff from the saddle.

"It's Aethermist, Julius."

Julius dropped from his horse, but not quickly enough. A loud demonic howl pierced our ears. The howl spooked our horses and they ran off.

Julius tried to grab the reins but they slipped past his grasp.

"Dammit!"

Another howl pierced the air. This time accompanied with a heavy snarl. Two figures skulked out of the mists. Their red eyes flickered in the fog. Large wolf-like beasts came into view. Instead of the fur I expected, they covered in a thick scaled hide. Large black fangs dripped blood onto the dirt below.

Julius turned to me with a serious look, "Keep your guard up. That damned horse took off with my shield." He frowned, "I won't be able to use any of my defensive skills without it."

"Noted, I will have to be a big girl and take care of myself. What's new?"

We took up our party positions. Though, with just the two of us it was more of a simple line formation.

Julius raised his sword and peered into the mists.

I brought my staff up and channeled magick through it. The mists around me were absorbed by the focus crystal.

"Source of light that dwells among the veiled. Come forth and guide our way, Radiance!"

Bright golden light washed over us and my rune pulsed with a notification.

» YOU ARE AFFECTED BY AN AURA OF LIGHT

In a quick flick of my wrist, I drew a small circular sigil in the air and channeled a small amount of energy through my hand.

"Let the power hidden within my being come forth, Brilliance!"

A violet flash of light cascaded down over me and another notification flashed.

» YOU ARE AFFECTED BY ARCANE BRILLIANCE

Julius was holding his sword squarely in front of him, casting an incantation of his own, "—cleanse my blade of impurities, Imbuement!

The weapon flashed brightly, dulling quickly to a golden glow along its sharp edge.

One of the demonic wolves leapt at me. Julius caught it in the side with his sword, the blade glanced against thick scales but knocked it off course.

The wolf snarled at him; its aggression successfully secured. Julius shouted out a shattering cry and the other wolf snarled and glared at Julius.

Nice taunt!

With the wolves' aggro held by Julius, I focused my magick and brought holy energy into my fist.

"Righteous Fire!"

A simple HOLY BOLT soared towards the wolf that lunged at me. The fiery bolt punctured through its scales and exploded with force. Chunks of flesh and hide laid strung out around the wounded body of the wolf, now struggling to rise up.

I tapped my rune to bring up a display and review the damage to the creature.

» BLADE SLASH [IMBUED] GLANCES, INFLICTING MODERATE (65) DAMAGE
» HOLY BOLT HITS, INFLICTING MODERATE (134) DAMAGE
» HOLY BOLT CAUSES MAJOR WOUNDS

Moderate damage, so these things are definitely Demons.

Julius brought his blade down with a killing blow and pierced the wolf's heart through the gaping wound. It went limp and the red glow of its eyes faded.

I'll take that as dead.

Julius and I both turned to the remaining wolf. It was still focused on him and lunged forwards.

Julius brought his sword in to parry—and was nearly knocked over by the weight of the beast.

Its claws tried to take hold, but couldn't find purchase. Julius squared his legs and pushed the wolf back.

"Rooarrh!" He let out a rage filled growl.

I called out to him.

"Julius, they're Demons. Keep its attention and I'll blow it apart with another bolt. Then you finish it off like that last one."

Julius nodded and brought his sword up in a striking stance. He leapt forward at the wolf and slashed at its snarling jowls. He struck true and the wolf yelped in pain.

No way he was losing its aggro to my spell casting now.

I brought another HOLY BOLT to bear and sent it flying at the wolf's side. Another explosion and more visceral bits sent flying across the battlefield.

» BLADE SLASH [IMBUED] HITS, INFLICTING MODERATE (122) DAMAGE
» HOLY BOLT HITS, INFLICTING MODERATE (147) DAMAGE
» HOLY BOLT CAUSES MAJOR WOUNDS

Julius brought his blade down and finished off the demon-wolf. Its body writhed on the dirt as its muscles convulsed. A low pained growl escaped its maw before the light in its eyes dulled.

He turned to me, his breath was heavy and labored. Long gashes were etched down the center of his breastplate. The damage to his chest armor was severe, but the gouged metal along his left bracer was even worse.

"Looks like that thing almost got you good. Are you alright, do you need healing?"

Even if he was injured, his stubborn ass wouldn't tell me. The impulse to attempt a block must have been pretty strong, though he probably felt pretty dumb for blocking with his arm.

I swiped over my rune and brought up a new display showing my party statistics.

PARTY MEMBERS	STATISTICS	VALUES
AIRIS VANIXI (OPERATOR)	HEALTH	50 / 50
	STAMINA	162 / 200
	MAGICKA	320 / 380
JULIUS ADAEMUS (INITIATOR)	HEALTH	487 / 500
	STAMINA	13 / 400
	MAGICKA	50 / 50

"I'm fine." he huffed. Still catching his breath.

Barely missing any health. Yeah, he'll live.

Performing that defensive parry really drained his stamina. It was more than common knowledge among defender-type class specializations, that using any guard skills without a shield can be devastating.

Julius leaned back on a tree and sheathed his blade. The aethermists fell back and rescinded into the forest.

With the way clear I should look for our horses. This will be an exhausting walk if we can't find them.

I let out a sharp whistle.

And... nothing. This has turned into a nightmare of a day. Alright, well looks like we're going to have to search around. But first those demon dogs.

I searched both corpses and collected what I could,

LOOTABLES

Item	Attributes	Description
DEMONIC FANG x4	-	Large black fangs of a demonic creature.
DEMONIC SCALE x65	-	Thick scaled plates of a demonic creature.

JULIUS
<INITIATOR>

AIRIS
<OPERATOR>

487/500

HP   50/50
         162/200   13/400

MP   320/380   50/50

It was possible we could use these scales to improve his armor. If not, we could always still sell them to an armorsmith if we come across one.

Julius was still resting against his tree. It would be quite a few minutes before his stamina recovered back to full. I'd let him rest for a while longer. Then we can go chase down our horses. Julius likely would be able to track them, he had a decently high perception attribute.

I leaned my back against another tree and let out one last sharp whistle to see if our horse would come running..

This time, instead of no response, I was met with another sharp whistle. Except this wasn't the whistle from a mouth, it was the whistle of an arrow that embedded itself in the tree four inches from my face.

"Ah!" I recoiled and flopped down, scurrying around the tree. "Julius! Take cover, archer!"

"Celestials above, are you kidding me?" Julius groaned, standing and drawing his sword. He spat on the ground.

"That was a warning shot, little miss," A man's voice called out from the woods. "Tell your bodyguard there to stand down and there won't be any trouble."

"..."

More of this bodyguard nonsense, huh.

I looked over at Julius, who was hunkered behind his tree with his sword at the ready.

"Hey, Julius."

"Yeah?"

"Mess this guy's day up for me, will ya'?"

"With pleasure."

"Oh come now, let's be reasonable shall we?" The man stepped into view. He was tall and slender. Much taller than a normal person, seven feet at the least. Straight white hair fell down along his face like needles. His face was obscured by a faceguard, but sharp pointed ears and striking golden eyes stuck out like a pearl in the mud. This was not a human, but a Noblebourne.

This Noblebourne was heavily geared, and his presence washed over me in an aura of intimidation. He wore a crimson-red full plate chestguard adorned with runes, with matching scaled pauldrons and plate greaves.

Who is this guy? Let's take a look.

I tapped my rune and a visual came into view.

TARGET		STATISTICS	VALUES
[HIDDEN]		HEALTH	150 / 150
		STAMINA	40 / 305
		MAGICKA	50 / 50

Well, damn.

He had some kind of magic hiding his identity. But he didn't seem to be magickally adept, judging by his low magicka value. Probably some sort of an enchantment on that armor.

"I want your gold, not your lives." He said in a sing-song melody, as he drew two slender blades from behind his back, "But I will take both if you don't comply."

Oh fun, a bandit.

Julius readied his blade and advanced. The bandit charged forward.

The two locked blades—but without his shield to block the second blade, Julius took a deep slash to his right leg. Blood sprayed down onto the dirt.

As they crossed swords, I began channeling magickal energy for a complex incantation. My hands glowed brightly as I traced out an intricate sigil in the space ahead of me.

"Vanguard of Heaven, In the light of divinity, I unleash my wrath and cull those who are judged, Righteous Fire!"

I had both hands pressed tightly together in a closed fist. As I finished my incantation, I flung them forward and a massive bolt of golden flame soared across the field. The HOLY BOLT impacted the bandit directly in the chest—and dissipated harmlessly...

What in the Aether!?

» HOLY BOLT IS ABSORBED [WARDING RUNE]

Shit. Damnable warding magick.

If my offensive spells weren't going to be effective, then this fight would be up to Julius.

Steel continued to clash. Julius' training as a military officer showed, as a well timed parry knocked a blade from the bandit's right hand.

Switching his remaining blade to his right hand, the bandit readied himself and lunged forward, swinging low. Another nasty hit to Julius' right leg.

Julius was now favoring his left, each step with a slight limp.

I sent a second HOLY BOLT at the bandit.

This bolt also dissipated harmlessly, but I aimed it so that it hit near his face. His steps faltered during the push off for a lunge. Even if I couldn't deal damage, I could annoy him with the blinding bright lights.

The blind allowed Julius to parry the fumbled attack and land a hit with a RIPOSTE. The attack struck deep into the bandit's right forearm.

That should put him on the defensive!

The bandit switched his blade back to his left hand. The right arm clearly crippled.

I channeled magick for two more HOLY BOLT spells, as Julius readied an attack skill. The first bolt dissipated but allowed Julius to lunge forward and deliver a slashing attack. The blade glanced off the bandit's breastplate. The second bolt though, exploded.

Looks like your wards were mostly for show.

» RIPOSTE [IMBUED] HITS, INFLICTING MINOR (38) DAMAGE
» BLADE SLASH [IMBUED] HITS, INFLICTING MINOR (22) DAMAGE
» HOLY BOLT IS ABSORBED [WARDING RUNE]
» STRIKE [IMBUED] HITS, INFLICTING MINOR (40) DAMAGE
» HOLY BOLT HITS, INFLICTING MINOR (42) DAMAGE
» HOLY BOLT CAUSES MAJOR WOUNDS

The explosive force of the bolt impacted on the bandit's faceguard.

"Maahhhrr..."

A bloody mist sprayed out as he cried out in pain. He fell backwards and his final blade dropped to the ground.

Julius limped forward, his steps fell as heavy as his breath.

He raised his blade weakly to finish off the bandit—

CLICK

Before his sword came down, a metallic noise echoed through the trees... followed by the sound of steel piercing flesh.

I watched in horror as Julius' body twisted around. He dropped awkwardly to his knees, his leg buckled and his body fell to its side. Blood poured from a wound in his chest.

Nonono! Julius—Oh shit!

I dropped my staff and ran forward, golden light already channeling through my fingers. A smooth wooden bolt was embedded in his breastplate. With a look of surprise and shock, he mouthed inaudibly to me. Kneeling beside him, I placed both hands over his chest and channeled the energy to him.

"Blessed and divine light, I pray to you. Bestow your warmth unto me and save this one from harm. Heal!"

But nothing happened...

Aggressively I swiped at my blinking rune.

» HEAL [MAJOR] FAILS [CRITICAL FAILURE], WOUND OBSTRUCTED

Celestials be damned, I am not letting Julius die. Not here. Not ever!

My voice broke, "It's going to be okay Julius. I've got you. I just need to remove," I indicated in a wide motion to his whole chest, "this. I have to clear the wound."

I pulled my dagger from my leg and cut the straps of his breastplate.

Holding the bolt as steady as possible I broke the shaft, and removed the front plate.

Blood was still pouring from the wound, it was impossible to see the extent of the damage.

Julius' gasped for air, and in a coughing fit blood sprayed from his mouth. Still conscious. He kept his gaze directly on me.

I mimed the action of pulling an arrow from my chest, "Julius, I'm going to take the arrow out. And then I'm going to heal the wound. I need you to stay awake."

I put extra emphasis on the last sentence, hoping that if he heard anything it would be that he couldn't drift off.

Julius nodded.

I think he nodded. One... Two... Three!

In the silent count of three to myself, I ripped the bolt head from his chest.

More blood, this time it was now spraying into the air. I focused my will, and with every fiber in my body I channeled all my magick into my hands. I placed my palms down against his chest again and forced the energy into the wound.

"Blessed and divine light, I pray to you. Grant me the power of your golden flame. Bestow your warmth unto me and save this one from harm. Heal!"

This time, the blood loss slowly came to a stop. The wounded flesh knitted back together; the traumatic damage reversed.

A dramatic gasp of air filled his lungs and he coughed more blood onto the ground.

» HEAL [MAJOR] INFLICTS EXTREME HEALING (637) [CRITICAL]

Thank the Celestials!

Julius let himself fall back into the dirt. He let out a nervous chuckle, which turned into full blown laughter. Contagious laughter. We both laid in the dirt laughing like a pair of lunatics.

"Ahh... that sucked." Julius finally groaned.

"Yeah."

"That bandit is dead, right?"

I looked at the bandit and swiped my rune.

TARGET		STATISTICS	VALUES
[HIDDEN] (DECEASED)		HEALTH	0 / 150
		STAMINA	0 / 305
		MAGICKA	0 / 50

"Extra dead. I blew his face off."

"Good... That guy was an ass."

"Yeah."

" ... "

" ... "

"I call dibs on the armor."

"You sure could use it," I chuckled, picking up the remains of his armor's front plate. I dangled it at Julius, "This set is out of commission."

"Give me a minute to catch my breath." he closed his eyes and let out a long sigh. "Actually, give me an hour."

I let Julius have his rest to search the Noblebourne's corpse—and remove his armor. A few steps past the tree line, I found a small burrow in the ground and pulled out a large knapsack and a satchel. The pack contained various meal rations and road supplies. The satchel was bulging with coins.

By the Aether, this... was a lot of money.

I wondered how many people had this miscreant attacked or robbed. This far out into the wilds, it's likely he prayed on Adventurers that were either heading into or leaving scattered dungeons and ruins.

What a complete bastard.

The Noblebourne were a race that appeared very human-like. Their origins dated back with the origin of Elves.

It's said they were the Celestial's favored race. That is, until they grew too arrogant. Some scholars believe the reason that Humans resemble the Noblebourne so closely is that we're the second try at the race.

Those same scholars also believe that given the human race's penchant for warfare, deceitfulness, and capacity for hate... that the Noblebourne must truly be demons when compared among the mortal races.

LOOTABLES

Item	Attributes	Description
SILVER COIN x235	currency	
GOLD COIN x52	currency	
WRIST CROSSBOW	17-20 Damage	A small wrist-mounted crossbow that is easy to conceal
PLATE CHESTGUARD (RUNE-BOUND)	+40 Armor +5 Toughness +5 Resolve	Ornately decorated exquisite plate armor. Adorned with spell-absorbing runes.
SCALE PAULDRONS	+15 Armor	Ornately decorated exquisite scale armor pauldrons
PLATE GREAVES	+10 Armor -1 Swiftness	Ornately decorated exquisite plate greaves.
STEEL KNIFE x10	35 – 45 Damage	A well-balanced throwing knife.
VANADIUM STEEL BLADE x2	55 – 67 Damage +2 Finesse +1 Reflex	High-quality alloy blade. Slender and lightweight.
STEEL BOLT x3	-	A slender steel broad-headed bolt for a small crossbow.

I dragged the bags and equipment back to Julius and threw it all down on the ground. I felt exhausted and took a place next to him on the soft dirt.

My rune blinked at me incessantly, I had a notification waiting for me.

» YOU HAVE GAINED IN POWER, YOUR ATTRIBUTES HAVE INCREASED:
» AETHER HAS INCREASED TO 21
  » INTELLIGENCE HAS INCREASED TO 35
  » WISDOM HAS INCREASED TO 24
  » SANITY HAS INCREASED TO 6
» VITALITY HAS INCREASED TO 19
  » RESOLVE HAS INCREASED TO 36
  » STAMINA HAS INCREASED TO 18

After his brief rest, and with a little bit of effort, we got Julius fitted and geared up in the new plated armor.

We picked up the tracks of our horses quickly, and after a chase-down, found them by a river.

After packing away our loot, I broke out some of our travel rations and nibbled on a bitter dried fruit bar.

THREE

BY NOON WE HAD REACHED THE CHECKPOINT Station.

Julius dismounted near a tree. He was mid way through kneeling down behind the tree when he stopped, walked back to his horse, and unlatched a buckle. His shield came loose from the saddle.

Good call, Julius.

I chuckled lightly at the dramatic way that he secured it to a fitting on his back.

Digging out a pair of binoculars from a belt pouch, he resumed kneeling behind the tree. After two minutes he gave me his verdict.

"It's abandoned."

"You're sure?"

"No patrols. No guards at all, actually. I'm sure."

We tied up our horses and made our way forward to scout the fort. In the center was a stone-brick barracks atop a hill, surrounded by eight bunkers. Each of those were sunken into the ground, with large earthwork fortifications winding around in front of them.

Two more permanent structures rose along the outpost's southern border. A tall wooden tower was built above a stone workshop and a large wooden stable. The entire encampment was encircled by eight foot palisade walls.

The place was definitely abandoned, the outpost commander must have received news of the coup. Without new orders from Axio, they probably set up camp somewhere out of sight.

I noticed dried and faded rectangular patches of grass along the western edge that seemed to indicate a large number of temporary structures, like tents. There were over thirty patches in total.

If they were tents, then there was a larger force than normal stationed here. The barracks would have been ample housing for anyone stationed here, with room for more than two-hundred Divisionals. With all those tents added in, the force here would have exceeded over five-hundred.

Julius called out to me from atop the tower. I jogged over to the workshop and waited for him to come down.

A loud crash echoed from inside the stone building and I heard Julius yell out something incoherent. He stumbled through the doorway, kicking an odd shaped metal object. When he looked up and saw me, a look of embarrassment spread across his face.

In an effort to prevent me from poking fun, he quickly pointed out past the camp's border.

"There's, uh... A break in the tree line over that way. It looked like it was cleared out to make room for wagons. My hunch is that the Divisionals are holed up a few miles in."

I eyed the direction his finger was pointing in and we headed off to the edge of the outpost. Just like he thought, there were cart-wheel spaced depressions worn in the grass leading into the forest.

As we were walking back to our horses, I pulled my coin from my pocket. I turned back to look at Julius and continued to step backwards, raising an eyebrow at him.

He sighed.

"Heads..."

I sent the coin spinning through the air.

It landed neatly on the back of my hand and I covered it with the other.

"If it's your call, what would your plan be?" I asked my irritated looking partner.

"I'd set up camp and light a fire near that break in the trees. I'm confident that they're running patrols through the woods, one of those patrols checks in the outpost to look for disturbances."

He paused to stretch his arms high above his head, letting out a long, dramatic, pained groan. "They find us, we play nice, and they take us to their new base. I'd also like to take advantage of the downtime to rest for a bit. I did get shot in the chest, remember?"

He smirked at me.

I pulled my hand back to reveal the face resting on the back of my hand. Tails. I smirked back at him.

"I'm sure you're right, that a patrol will come by sooner or later—but I don't want to risk the later part being too long, and have someone else notice a signal fire."

I tilted my hand back to show him the red-stained wings on the face of the coin. His eyes rolled.

"I think we'll head into the forest and find them ourselves." I slowed my back-stepping pace to allow Julius to catch up and I placed my hand over his chestplate, "How's it feeling?"

"I'm fine." He batted my hand away instinctively—his face softened instantly, "I really am fine. I'm sorry for that."

We mounted up and rode past the borderline of the outpost and dense forest. Julius stared longingly at the treeline as we passed by. I knew he was tired, but we could rest once we were in the safety of the new camp.

The terrain was not particularly kind to the Divisional wagons, as we passed four of them off the trailway, their wheels splintered and broken.

We rode for over an hour through the forest. Julius spotted the massive earthworks barricade a second before I did, his arm shot up in a tight fist at his shoulder's level. We both pulled on our reins and came to a stop.

A small break in the treeline was ahead of us. The sun was still high enough in the sky that we could plainly see a field of green grass interrupted by the dusky tones of dirt piled up high. Tall cut timbers formed a wall behind the earthen trenches. We dismounted, moving closer on foot to get our bearings and do a little recon.

We were still about a thousand feet away from the structure.

"What are the chances they let us in the front do—" Julius cut himself off when a loud snap popped behind us.

I tried to spin around quickly. But as I turned, someone pushed me backwards and I fell down into a bushy growth.

Can today just be over already!?

I cried out in surprise when I hit the ground, a tough branch had left a cut across my leg during the fall.

A sword flashed in front of my face and the feeling of cold steel pressed against my neck.

"Don't even think about moving," a voice said dryly. A loud whistle came from the forest. It echoed sharply through the woods, and was followed by the sounds of heavy steps running our direction.

I looked up at the person whose sword was threatening my life, and was relieved to see they were wearing the standard red and white uniform of the Vanixian Republic. She was in a mix of heavy and medium armor, a steel breastplate with leather pauldrons. I couldn't make out her rank, as her body was turned away from me to keep an eye on Julius.

"Who in the Aether are you?" she demanded.

"Get that sword off her neck or you'll regret it!" Julius snarled.

Celestials above, he's going to get us killed. 'Play nice and they'll take us to their base', he had said just an hour ago.

In response, a man appeared behind him. A plated fist contacted the back of Julius' head, dropping him to the ground. Julius let out a groan of pain.

The man stepped into view and knelt down in front of me. He was wearing a full-plate uniform with Knight-Lieutenant's insignias painted around the collar plate. "You want to be more cooperative? Or maybe you want to eat some dirt, like your friend here." he sneered.

I needed to come up with something quick to defuse this situation.

"Maybe, you'd like to explain why you've assaulted a superior officer." I tilted my head slowly in a nod towards Julius, who was now struggling against two others, "and why you're threatening a Commander?"

The Lieutenant glanced over at Julius and motioned for his men to pull him up. Julius' insignia were easy to see in the sunlight through the canopy above.

The Lieutenant looked back at me, his expression now more stressed. The woman holding me at sword point shifted uneasily and looked to the man for direction.

"That is High-Protector Julius Adaemus." I said plainly, "And I am Commander Airis Vanixi."

The Lieutenant stiffened, his face went from stressed to outright distraught.

I hope that did the trick.

He opened his mouth to speak but hesitated for a moment. He cleared his throat and choked out, "That's impossible. Commander Airis was killed in action."

"I was not."

"..."

He stared blankly at me. What kind of response do you give to that kind of logic? The woman at his side responded instead.

"You could be spies!" She cried out, and then pushed her sword closer to my neck, "You don't even have a uniform on."

Julius interjected, "Yep, that's us. Two spies, who've come all this way through the forest and then decided to just walk up to your gates."

"Makes us some pretty poor spies," I jumped in, "We're here to see Commander Hailey Brooks."

The Lieutenant continued to stare at us, his eyes darted around between my face and Julius'. His shoulders finally relaxed and he sighed deeply, "Pearson, at ease. Lower your weapon and let her up." He then turned to Julius, "Tori, Garrett, let him go."

Julius was released and he jumped away from his two captors. He shook his arms and narrowed his eyes at them.

The Lieutenant looked back to me, "Your faces look familiar. I've seen both of your portraits at Command. So you're both either really good imitations or you're the real deal. Considering posing as two of the highest ranked members of our Republic to sneak into a base would be an idiotic idea, I'll take you to see the Commander. She'll recognize you if you really are who you claim to be."

"Great," I said as I struggled up from my leafy seat, "You know us, now how about we know you?"

The Lieutenant's arm snapped to a salute, his right arm resting against his chest, "I am Knight-Lieutenant Luke Mitchell. Vice Commander of the Third Divisionals."

He pointed down the row of his party, who had fallen in behind him, "These are the rest of my patrol party, You've met Knight Murphy Pearson." his finger pointing at the woman whose sword had moments ago been digging into my skin.

"Adept Abigail Garrett and Initiate Alexander Tori" he pointed at the two who were wrestling with Julius.

"Crusader Mei Devins, Knight Aeko Monroe, and finally Adept Tatsuko Hirota" He took in a deep breath. "You can pester them for their life stories back in camp if you'd like, but we should get a move on. We're past our check-in time and the guards at the gate get... worried, if we're late."

I gave everyone a smile and an awkward wave. They looked exhausted, any pleasantries could wait until we got back to their camp. I wasn't sure how to greet a party of soldiers that a moment ago were bearing arms down at us anyway.

"Lead the way Knight-Lieutenant."

We walked across the field with the scouting party. Julius held the reins to both our horses while I walked in the lead with Mitchell. I asked him questions about the state of things as we walked. He was reluctant to answer anything that pushed the boundary of Divisional operations, but I was persistent and got a few answers.

Julius made small talk with a few members in the scouting party. They seemed like good people. He even got a few of them to laugh.

We passed the earthwork checkpoint without any issues, the few men stationed there gave Julius and I odd looks but with Mitchell leading us on they went about their duties. Another hundred yards past the checkpoint and we came across another barricade, this one was much bigger and had large guard towers erected behind the walls.

As we neared the gates, a siren call rang out. The bustle of people running inside and the 'thump' of something heaving bracing against the wooden gate echoed through the open field.

A woman's voice yelled out from atop one of the towers, "Halt! Identify yourselves!"

Mitchell let out a sigh and looked up towards the guard tower, "Hanna, it's Luke. We're back, and we need to see the Commander. We've got a situation."

"It's patrol group seven, open the gate." she called down to somebody below. "I said open the gate! Now!"

Mitchell wasn't kidding about them getting worried if they were late, this woman was absolutely flustered.

The gate swung open and we were met by twelve fully armed guardsmen. Hanna had come down from her post atop the tower, and was running towards Mitchell.

"Luke! I was worried when you didn't come back on time—you're an hour late! Are you hurt? What kind of situation? Who are these two? What happened out there?" she rattled off questions in rapid fire.

Mitchell's hands were up in defense, "Woah, Hanna, slow down," he pointed at me, "This is Commander Airis Vanixi." He then pointed at Julius, "And this is her second-in-command, High Protector Julius Adaemus.

Hanna snapped to attention her arm raised to her chest in salute, the guardsmen behind her mimicking the actions.

"At ease everyone," I gave a salute back with an awkward smile, "No need for all the formalities right now. We really need to see your commander."

Mitchell continued, "We spotted them on our way back from patrol and followed them through the forest. We confronted them just before the clearing. I'm sorry for the delay."

Hanna looked at Mitchell, "Did you need one of us to escort them or are you and your party taking them?"

"Don't worry about it, I'll take them. I want to see the look on Hailey's face when she finds out Commander Vanixi has risen from the dead." He flashed a smirk back to me, "She was the one who told us that you fell in battle after all."

The gate closed behind us and the guards went back to their posts. Hanna walked with us for a while, and once we were out of guard's line of sight, she wrapped herself around Mitchell in a hug.

"You're not allowed to be late again, I was worried something had happened to you, Luke." Her voice was muffled, her face buried in his chest.

"I said I was sorry," Mitchell patted Hanna's head and hugged her back, "Now you gotta let me go Hanna, I really don't think Commander Vanixi would like to wait any longer to see Hailey."

"Of course, I'm sorry for keeping you Commander. Please keep an eye on Luke for me. Don't let him cause you any trouble with Hailey."

Hanna started back to the gate post. I looked at Mitchell with a raised eyebrow. The scouting party members all looked away and pretended they didn't see anything.

His hands fidgeted and his eyes darted around.

"We… Uh, we're all childhood friends. Hanna, the Commander, and I."

"Hey, I didn't say anything." I laughed.

Divisional regulations didn't lay out specific guidelines on professional conduct. Some officers made it a big deal if you called a superior officer by their first name, but it was mostly because they were nobles. The noble classes in Axio often got uppity and offended when 'commoners' addressed them by their first names.

"It's refreshing to be around people who aren't so wrapped up in silly city etiquette."

Mitchell gave me a knowing smile and we followed the rest of the group that had walked up a small hill.

Reaching the top I saw the rest of the camp. A sea of canvas tents filled the large clearing. There were hundreds of people moving about their business.

This is insane, there are way more people here than I thought.

A few large tents were scattered about, Mitchell pointed them out as we walked towards the center; a Medical Bay, a Mess Hall, and a Blacksmith.

"There is an Artificer at the blacksmith, a Dwarven lass, goes by Dörien. She's a very skilled craftsman. She was with some refugees that joined us when we fled Axio."

We passed by a makeshift stable on our way in and turned over our horses. I grabbed my pack and slung it over my shoulder. Julius grabbed his as well, but then must have decided against lugging around the heavy thing because he left it with the stable attendant.

Our group finally arrived at a large tent that was smack dab in the center of the camp. Noticeably, there were a few guards stationed around this tent. Mitchell stopped and talked with one of the guards near the entrance. He pointed at us and the guard's eyes locked on to me. The guard gave a salute and Mitchell motioned for us to follow him in.

"They're in a meeting right now. Apparently it has been going on for about three hours."

Mitchell flashed a hand signal and his party members dispersed as we entered the tent.

Inside there was a large crude timber table and a number of chairs and stools, all with occupants. A cherry-red haired woman sat at one end. She was silently glaring at the others seated at the table, who were arguing loudly over each other.

Should we try and get her attention somehow?

Julius ribbed his elbow into my side and whispered, "Want me to call her over for you?"

I let out a quiet squeak and moved to put myself behind him.

"N-No... We can wait for them to finish up."

He glanced down at me and raised an eyebrow.

"What's up with you?"

"Nothing is up with me!" I hissed back at him.

The meeting members were too engrossed in their yelling match to notice us. I tuned Julius out, before he could start to tease me, focusing on the meeting going on instead.

"There are barely enough rations to last another three weeks! We need to organize new hunting and foraging parties."

"Bah, rations are the least of our problems if we don't get our hearths stocked with something heartier than these pines. We'll freeze before starving to death."

"The medical bay is at capacity looking after the sick and wounded, we need to be mindful of work shifts to not over tax our population. People are stressed beyond their limits!"

"We don't have enough raw iron to equip the initiates who have enlisted from the refugee pool. We have men and women whose duty armaments are made of wood."

"We don't have the manpower or resources to form a survey team to look for ore deposits. We'll just have to repurpose some nonessentials, like cutlery, and make hardened spearheads."

And so continued the needs and gripes of a makeshift camp...

Hailey's gaze drifted over our direction during a lull, her eyes moved right past me, hiding behind Julius in my rugged leather outfit and messy appearance, locking onto him. Her face twisted in puzzlement.

Julius' gaudy officer's uniform screamed 'look at me' with its golden trim. Paired with the crimson red armor he was wearing now—he stuck out in a crowd.

Her eyes grew wide when she recognized him. Julius slowly and calmly pointed at me, her gaze followed.

Hailey let out a high-pitched squeal, nearly falling out of her seat.

The others gathered at the table all fell silent and stared at her, as she was now trying to squirm out of her seat.

She freed herself and yelled, "Meetings over!"

A few of the attendees tried to voice their disapproval of the abrupt end, but the dissenters were met with a death glare, "I said, the meeting is over."

Nobody wasted any time shuffling out of the tent.

Hailey ran full speed into me, sending us both tumbling to the ground.

"Gaaah!"

I reached out to Julius in an attempt to stop my descent, but as I fell backwards a wicked grin spilled across his face.

We hit the earthen floor with a thud and I let out a pitiful groan.

Hailey's exuberant smile and rosy-pink eyes filled my view. She grabbed my hands and exclaimed, "You're not dead! You survived! And you're here!"

I stared up at her as she continued rambling. After the excitement for my miraculous return faded enough for her to regain some composure; she turned her attention to Julius. She began a rapid fire beratement session, blaming him for letting me be captured.

Her arms flailed as she cursed up a storm. I was still pinned to the ground and was starting to get my senses back.

Hailey was straddling me at my waist, jostling around wildly while arguing with Julius. Overtaken with embarrassment I closed my eyes and tried not to make any noise.

Nnnnnngh!

"Hey, Airis. Why's your face look like that?"

My eyes popped open and Julius was peering down at me.

Hailey had stopped squirming around and was looming over me as well. "Are you okay? You look really red—You're not getting sick are you!?"

"N-no! It's not that, it's—nevermind! Just let me up!"

She hurried off of me and Julius reached out a hand. I glared at him with narrowed eyes. I swatted it out of the way and scrambled up on my feet by myself.

"Is your face stuck in that weird look now or something?" He turned to Hailey, "I think you might have broken her with that tackle."

"My face isn't broken, Julius!"

I huffed and stomped away from him.

Hailey followed after me and jumped ahead of me. A great big smile was spread across her face.

"I really am happy to see you."

She took a step back and looked me over. "But, Commander, you're out of uniform." She teased. She placed her arms on her hips and her smile turned to a smirk, "That is so unlike you."

"Well, you see," I raised my arms in playful defense, "the guards down at the prison didn't give me a chance to change before we left Axio. Also, the service there was terrible. I wanted to leave a review but Julius was adamant that we left in a hurry."

She paused to take in my excuse and started giggling, "I guess I'll accept that as an answer."

She let herself laugh for a moment, but then let her arms fall, "I am so glad you're safe. I thought you were dead!"

"Yeah, I heard that. From your man over there actually." I pointed to Mitchell, who was now slowly backing out of the tent, "It made for a rather tense first impression."

Hailey peaked around me, "Oh, Luke! I didn't even see you were here. You found Airis on your patrol? That certainly is lucky."

Mitchell stopped moving, but wouldn't make eye contact with Hailey, "It's more like she found us really. We, uh... stopped them just before one of the checkpoints."

Hailey stepped around me and glared up at Mitchell.

"Luuuuke. What did you do? Why won't you look at me?"

With an exasperated look, he twisted towards me, then to Julius, then back to me. He finally settled with his down facing Hailey. One arm came up over his shoulder and he let out a deep exhale.

"You said she was dead. So when some lady comes trampling through the woods claiming to be Commander Airis Vanixi, Pearson may have inferred that she could have been a spy... And she may have also pointed a sword at her neck."

Hailey continued to glare at Mitchell.

A single bead of sweat raced down his face.

"..."

Hailey finally broke the tension, "Well, she isn't wearing a uniform. And I thought she was dead... So I guess it makes sense you wouldn't believe her. But what kind of idiotic spies would try to impersonate two of the highest ranking members of our Divisionals? That's just silly."

"Uh, yeah. I had that thought as well. It was a long day, and following them through the forest put us off schedule by an hour."

"Ooooooh you were late to check back in? Did Hanna rally the troops and race into the forest to save you?" Hailey chuckled.

"She did not."

Julius let out a cough.

"But it looked like she was pretty close to it, though." I chimed in, "They were geared up and ready when we came through that gate."

"That's our Hanna for you." Hailey replied.

Hailey looked at Mitchell with a big grin, "Luke, why don't you take Julius and square away a tent for these two. Set it up near mine—make sure it's a nice one."

"Will do. I'll come find you once we get it setup."

Mitchell and Julius left the command tent. Hailey fell back into her chair at the table and let out a long drawn out sigh.

"That bad here, huh?"

"We have more problems than solutions, it seems. We're a Divisional Army, not a logistics committee. I just don't have answers for problems, unless I can cast a spell at it to fix it."

"It sounds like most of the issues are mundane in the grand scheme of things. I'm just guessing, but that group was probably all nobles? They like to squawk about problems and make them seem much larger than they truly are."

Hailey pondered for a minute, her finger tapping her chin. "They are all nobles." She stopped tapping and pointed her finger at me, "But hey, we're nobles too ya' know. I don't squawk."

"I don't squawk either, but that's because we're a different breed than the political noble houses."

"Yeah, you have a point there," she got up and grabbed my hand, "Come on, I'll show you around! We can get you something more fitting than those street clothes and leather wrappings."

Hailey led me around the camp, introducing me to everyone we passed by.

This woman is crazy, how are you on a first name basis with hundreds of people?

Everyone seemed like they were in good spirits. The camp had a large training area laid out with an endurance and agility course. There were some guardsmen practicing attacks against dummies with wooden swords.

Recalling one of the issues from the meeting, I thought those could likely be their duty weapons, and not just training weapons.

We finally stopped at one of the large tents. This tent was different from the others, it encircled a stone structure and smoke could be seen rising from the center. It was surrounded by a few wagons that were packed with crates. The clang of metal rang out from the tent.

"This is our supply depot and blacksmith. If we're gonna get you outfitted, this is the place."

Hailey stepped inside.

I hesitated for a moment, but followed in after her.

In front of me was a large makeshift smeltery and forge. Two figures were working around the forge. A dark haired woman wearing a thick leather apron and a face mask. And a short, stout woman with long copper colored hair and goggles on her face.

I'm guessing that's the dwarf Mitchell was talking about earlier.

She looked up and waved at us. "Heya, Hailey. Who ye' got there wit' ya'?"

"Heya, Dori, this is Commander Airis Vanixi, the lady that made it possible for all of us to escape Axio during the insurrection." Hailey turned to me, "Airis, this is Dörien the Artificer."

Dörien put down her hammer and pulled her goggles up on her head. "Aye? This 'ers the lassie then. Nice ta' meet ya'."

The clang of hammer swings continued behind her as the other woman was still working. Dörien turned around and shouted at her, "Oi! Ye' just gonnae sit back there an' ignore Hailey?"

The woman gave two final swings of her hammer and lifted the steel she was working on up to inspect it. She then quenched it in a water barrel and walked over to us. She pulled down her facemask, "Afternoon Commander, and... guest? Haven't seen you around before."

"Hi Rhia, this is Commander Airis. She was the one who stayed behind during the retreat from Axio."

"Oh is that so? I heard you were dead—actually come to think of it... Hailey, you were the one who told me she was dead." Rhia gave Hailey a scowling look.

"Aye, ye' did tell us the lassie was dead."

Hailey let out an awkward chuckle, "Heh, well turns out I was wrong."

"It's nice to meet you both." I gave a quick wave and nudged Hailey, "She told me you might be able to get me equipped in something a bit more suiting. I pieced together what was available, and you can see what I've currently got isn't anything great."

"Actually, you may be in luck."

Rhia got close to me. Personal levels of close. She started looking me over. She grabbed my upper arm and forearm, and started squeezing.

"Oh yeah, you're gonna be just perfect. I just finished the steel for a longsword. Nice quality blade, going to be a twenty strength requirement once I'm finished. Which is too high for most of the folks needing to be geared up."

Hailey clapped excitedly, "Wonderful! A sword works for you right, Airis?"

"I, uh..." I stammered.

I could use something a bit more close and personal. Especially if I found myself in another situation like this morning. Julius would probably appreciate it if I could back him up with a blade when things get dicey.

"Yeah, a sword would be perfect."

I'll just have Julius run me through some pointers and maybe I can learn a skill or two from him with enough training.

"Great! Oh, and Dori," Hailey poked at Dörien, "would you be able to spice it up with some of your E and E talents?"

E and E, what in the Aether is that?

"Aye, ye' just let me know what kindae enchants yer' lookin' fer'. An' if ye' got any materials for 'em."

I was puzzled. But Dörien was looking to me for a reply.

"Oh, uhm... I don't think I have anything like that on me. I don't even know the first thing on what kind of enchants you'd even be able to put on a sword."

Rhia was heading back to the forge but turned back, She must have noticed the look of bewilderment on my face because she explained it for me, "Well, Dori specializes in fire and earth enchants and enhancements. So if you had any materials that are aligned with those elements she could imbue the blade with it."

I pulled my pack around and set it down on a table. A little bit of digging and I produced the fangs and scales from the demon-wolves.

"Would these work, or are there too few of them to do anything?"

Dörien put her goggles back over her eyes and inspected a fang closely. She put it back on the table and tapped it a few times with her finger.

"Hmmm."

She grabbed her hammer and slammed it down on one of the fangs. I flinched, expecting shards of fang to fly out everywhere. But there was not even a scratch on the fang.

"Aye, these'll work."

Rhia was back at her station and was working on the blade steel. Dörien took the fangs and scales and went over to her station and started scrawling something on a piece of parchment.

Hailey led me out of the tent.

"Let's give them some time to work on that for you. We can plunder some of the crates outside for armor and get you fitted into something nice."

We scrounged through the top crate, and after about forty minutes we found a single bracer that looked like it would be a good fit.

Searching all of these crates on our own was going to be excruciating.

Hailey answered my unspoken call for help by calling over some soldiers who were passing by. She suckered them into our endeavor. A few crates later, one giant mess of equipment, and another hour's time; I had a full set of new armor.

Hailey helped get me fitted in a small tent nearby and we put my old gear in a drop-off crate for the blacksmith staff to take a look and see if it was worth salvaging.

LOOTABLES

Item	Attributes	Description
EMBOSSED LEATHER TUNIC	+28 Armor +3 Toughness +2 Finesse	A high-quality supple leather tunic with decorative wings on the chest, and golden trim.
STEEL CHESTPLATE	+45 Armor +5 Toughness	A high-quality steel chestguard with matching pauldrons.
EMBOSSED LEATHER BOOTS	+12 Armor +1 Swiftness	A high-quality pair of boots with great gripping tread.
STEEL-BRACED WRISTGUARDS	+15 Armor +1 Reflex	Fine leather wristguards with plated bracers.
DAMASK GLOVES	+5 Armor	Fine silk weave gloves.
DAMASK BLOUSE	+5 Armor	A fine silk weave blouse.
STEEL-BRACED LEGGUARDS	+15 Armor +1 Reflex	Fine leather leggings with plated legguards.
EMBOSSED LEATHER BELT	+1 Finesse +2 Reflex	A high-quality leather belt with a golden buckle and attachment for a scabbard.

"So, what do you think Hailey? Do I look like a respectable Commander now?" I strutted around a little bit, and flashed her a wicked grin.

"You certainly look closer to the part. Oh, I should have a spare uniform and set of insignias back in my tent, I can give them to you tonight. Then it'll be official." She gave me a wink, "Let's go check in with Dori and Rhia."

Hailey grabbed my arm and led me back into the blacksmith's tent.

Dörien was leaning over her workstation fidgeting with a strange tool. Laying across the table was a long angled blade. Its hilt consisted of an extraordinarily long handle that was wrapped tightly in a grooved black-leather, a slender angled pommel, and was missing a guard. The hilt was a dark ebony black, that looked like it absorbed the light around it.

The blade of the sword had the same ebony color through the first half on the back of the blade, and then was elegantly given way to a dark gray steel edge along the flat at the midway point. The tip came to a point with a sharp angled curve. The entire blade arced very subtly from the pommel to the tip in an almost unnoticeable 'S' curve.

Rhia hovered over Dörien like a gargoyle, her eyes were glued to the blade. Hailey and I crept closer, trying not distract them from their sword crafting ritual.

Dörien shouted something I couldn't understand, then brought a long metal stamping tool out. With one of the fangs in her hand she channeled some magick until it glowed a bright red, she then placed it onto the blade, lining up the stamping tool. She brought a hammer out and struck the metal stamp down onto the fang.

A brilliant flash of light spilled through the tent followed by a loud high-pitched ringing. Hailey and I both brought our arms up to cover our ears but the ringing didn't lessen in its intensity.

Dörien laughed with wild abandon.

"No use in ye' tryin' to stop tha' ringin' there Commanders."

The light faded down and the ringing stopped.

Rhia was now practically drooling over the sword, which had taken on a dark crimson glow. Blood-red runes were etched along the flat of the blade. Their glow pulsated down the edge in a breathing rhythm.

Rhia's hands trembled over the blade.

"It's... perfect!" she looked up and saw Hailey and I, "Oh good you're back—with great timing." She motioned for us to come forward, "Come on, take a look! I already sharpened the blade before Dori did her thing, so it's ready to go. Give it a swing."

I looked down at the blade, measuring the handle size with my eyes. I grasped the blade with both hands.

It was incredibly light, but the balance felt off. I switched stance and held it in just my left hand.

That's much better.

The handle was long but the sword had been balanced to definitely be a one-handed blade.

I raised the blade up and swung out in front of me. My arm felt a strange pressure build up, and without any warning—the back of the blade erupted in a dark-crimson flame.

"Eeep!"

I let out a yelp in surprise and the three others jumped behind the workstation for cover as I stood there holding a burning sword.

Oh wow! What do I do? Is this going to burn down the tent?

I looked over at the three women for help. But wasn't met with any. Hailey cowered behind Dörien, who was behind Rhia.

Rhia's eyes were wide in amazement. She stared at the sword and whispered.

"It's... incredible."

"Aye, It's a masterpiece 'alright. But doncha' be burnin' down ma' forge!" Dörien exclaimed.

Hailey remained silent, in awe of the glowing flames.

I inspected the blade with a tap of my wrist. Maybe there was something about the weapon's attributes or details that will help me handle it.

LOOTABLES

ITEM	ATTRIBUTES	DESCRIPTION
CRIMSON BLADE	85-157 Damage +10 Sanity	An exquisite tempered steel blade imbued with demonic fire. When wielded, it ignites in SOULFIRE. Bound.

Woah!

The stats on this weapon were incredible. The master smiths in Axio could make items like this, but they would cost a fortune. This sword could be worth more than most noble's manors.

It looked like the flames were activated when the blade was wielded. So maybe if I just set the sword down... I gently set the sword on the workstation and the flames subdued.

"Phew!"

I wanted to find out what the SOULFIRE effect did. It sounded interesting. And I wasn't sure what it meant by 'Bound'. I tapped my rune and a new visual came into view.

SPELL	SCHOOL	CLASS	DESCRIPTION
SOULFIRE	Fire	Combat	Items affected by this spell are engulfed in a powerful flame. Attacks will deal splashing damage to nearby foes. Critical strikes have a chance to apply a curse that ignites the target's nerves; causing extreme damage.

"Ooooo..."

I was practically drooling while reading the dancing words on the interface. Hailey placed a hand on my shoulder and waved a hand in front of my face.

"Airis, is everything alright?"

She snapped me out of my trance.

"What? Yeah, it's just... this weapon is beyond incredible." I turned around to look at the two responsible. "Really, it's incredible. I can't thank you enough for this. It's leagues above what I was imagining."

Rhia bowed sincerely, "No, thank you! If it wasn't for you, Dori and I would be trapped in that city... Or worse."

"That'll do a 'ell of a lot more damage than tha' splinter on 'yer back."

I chuckled, "It sure will. I truly appreciate your work."

The doorway to the blacksmith's tent came open and Mitchell and Julius stepped inside.

"Ahh, we finally found you." Mitchell called out. He walked over to Hailey and after saying something quietly, they stepped outside.

Julius came over to me and let out a whistle.

"Looking like a proper Commander there, Airis. Nice to see you in something that isn't so ragged. The Knight-Lieutenant and I got a tent and..."

His voice trailed off when he got close enough to see the blade laying on the table

"...and—what is that!?"

"Oh, this? Just my new favorite thing in this world. Sorry Julius, you've been replaced."

I picked the Crimson Blade back up and gave it a quick slash through the air, sending the dark flames into a rage. Julius stared for a while and finally mouthed a single word.

"Fantastic."

"Commander, would you come here a moment?" Rhia called out from her workstation. She brought up a dark-scaled scabbard, strapping it onto the attachment fittings on my belt.

"I used the scales you brought with you. They should be resistant enough to the flame that it will be safe to sheathe your blade."

LOOTABLES

Item	Attributes	Description
DEMON SCALE SCABBARD	Fire Resistance	A high-quality sword scabbard made from demonic scales.

In awe of the blacksmith's work once more, I bowed to her in appreciation.

"Again, Rhia. I am incredibly thankful for your work."

I sheathed the blade and the flames rescinded once again. I looked at Julius, who still looked a little awestruck, and motioned for us to leave.

Hailey and Mitchell were still talking, but upon seeing us emerge from the tent cut their conversation short.

"Airis, I have to go take care of a situation with the Consulate members. I guess they didn't appreciate me sending them all away earlier, and a few of them have been causing a scene at the command tent. Give me a few hours to get things calmed down, meet me there?"

"Sure thing, Hails, no worries. I'll show Julius around some of the places you led me through, so he can get his bearing on the camp."

We departed and I walked Julius back through the camp. There were a lot more people around this time, the sun was starting to go down and the camp residents were settling down for the night. I elected to forgo any introductions with the camp residents to Julius. The both of us weren't social creatures afterall.

As we approached the training area Julius stopped me.

"Hey, If you're really eager to get a chance to use that new sword of yours. We can give your sword skills a little practice."

It wasn't that I didn't focus on combat skill training. It had more to do with my administration duties, that always outweighed any need to train in martial weapons.

I had some basic courses while in the Academy at least.

I nodded my head at Julius in agreement.

"They could use it. It's a good thing I know a really great swordsman."

A smirk grew on Julius' face and he let out a light laugh, "Yeah, yeah. I'm sure you already had planned to ask me to show you some 'cool sword skills', huh."

"So what if I did," I stuck my tongue out at him, "You are my best friend. You'd never say no to me."

The training site was cleared out, save for a few guards. We found a small area near a free wooden dummy and he began to show me some basic stance poses and a slash attack.

After an hour, I felt as if I was about to collapse. My breathing was heavy, my arms ached, and I was drenched in sweat. I slumped against a tree stump nearby and sent a mental call.

I'm ready for death. Take me now, Gemini. I'm ready— Julius threw a water canteen at me.

As I hydrated and waited for my breathing to catch up, I reviewed my new notifications.

» YOU HAVE GAINED IN POWER, YOUR ATTRIBUTES HAVE INCREASED:
» STRENGTH HAS INCREASED TO 25
   » TOUGHNESS HAS INCREASED TO 8
» VITALITY HAS INCREASED TO 23
   » ENDURANCE HAS INCREASED TO 9
   » STAMINA HAS INCREASED TO 26
» AGILITY HAS INCREASED TO 9
   » SWIFTNESS HAS INCREASED TO 12
   » PERCEPTION HAS INCREASED TO 6
   » REFLEX HAS INCREASED TO 11
» DEXTERITY HAS INCREASED TO 27
   » FINESSE HAS INCREASED TO 8
» YOU HAVE GAINED IN POWER, YOU HAVE LEARNED NEW SKILLS:
» NEW ACTION CLASS COMBAT SKILL, BATTLE STANCE
» NEW ACTION CLASS COMBAT SKILL, BLADE SLASH

"Great work. You'll be a master swordswoman in no time."

Julius hadn't broken a sweat at all, even though he was doing the same work I was doing. I had a ways to go before I could call myself a master anything. In between breaths I managed to get out a mangled word.

"T—thanks..."

When we arrived at the command tent we were assaulted by the pleasant fragrance of fresh bread and an unplaceable spicy aroma.

We greeted the guards and were told that Hailey had finished her meeting so we were welcome to head inside.

The meeting table had been converted into a dining table, complete with a large covering cloth and silverware. A meal had already been prepared. From the meaty smell, it was likely wild game brought in from the hunting parties.

It smells good, whatever it is.

Hailey was fussing over the placement of a candelabra with one of the attendants when she noticed us come in.

"Airis! Good you're back! Take a seat and dig in! I'm sure you're hungry and—Oh, you're filthy."

Her face went from cheerful to worried in a split second.

With a quick gesture another attendant brought over a wash basin and a towel.

My cheeks flushed with embarrassment and I gave my face a quick scrub.

"Less of a mess?"

"Much better!" she clapped her hands, "Now dig in, we have a lot to discuss after dinner."

FOUR

TENSE. THAT WAS THE ONLY WORD THAT sprung to mind to describe the atmosphere tonight.

The command tent was filled with the senior members of our broken Republic. Hailey called for this assembly after bringing Julius and I up to speed about the camp over dinner. We went over some light details on my plan to retake the city of Tolin, and she insisted that she bring everyone important in.

All of those 'everyones' were now making hushed small talk while we waited for Hailey and Mitchell to show up. They had left a few minutes ago to get one final person, who they insisted should attend because she had helped solve some important issues in the camp.

I recognized almost everyone in the room, save a few members of Hailey's Divisionals in attendance.

Standing around the central table were two members of the Consulate Court, Yenifer Lewis and Liam Byrant. Along with them were four Ministers, Jacob Hay, the Minister of Agriculture. Hannah Fuller, Minister of Justice. Yuji Tsuki, Minister of Health. Ridwan Bashir, Minister of State.

These were the same people in the meeting that our arrival interrupted...

Whoops.

Not like the Consul ever gets much done anyway, So I was sure it made no meaningful difference that we pushed their meeting back.

Scattered around the rest of the room were a few members of Mitchell's scouting party, Mei Devins, Aeko Monroe, and Murphy Pearson. Hanna Vynn was also present, though she looked disinterested and had found a seat along the back wall and was chatting with some other people I didn't know.

A silence fell over the room as Hailey returned. She and Mitchell entered with a small girl following behind them. I couldn't really see her from across the room, her head was down and her face was obscured by a hooded cloak. Mitchell and the mystery girl stopped just past the entryway and a small group of heavily armored guards took position just behind him, preventing any entrance to the tent.

Or exit, for that matter.

Hailey took her place at the head of the table and made an announcement.

"This call-to-order is designated as highly-restricted. All members are sworn to keep any details discussed here to themselves."

She kept her serious demeanor and continued, "Anyone who does not adhere to this will be punished under Divisional Doctrine judication to the highest degree."

She relaxed her shoulders and took a deep breath, "I understand that some members here are not fully familiar with Divisional practices and the restrictive lifestyle that comes with our service. But these are times of great strife and to maintain order all of you are going to have to learn quick and follow orders."

That last part was aimed at the consulate and other civilian members in attendance.

She took her seat and placed her arms in her lap, "With that out of the way, please be seated. At ease."

I took a seat next to Hailey. Julius took one across from me, facing the tent's entrance.

Hailey gave me a glance before beginning again, "Some of you may have been present when she first arrived, but I'd like to formally acknowledge the presence of Commander Airis Vanixi—"

A loud clatter rang out as something metal hit the floor, followed by a loud gasp of surprise.

I turned around to find the source of the interruption. The small girl that had arrived with Hailey and Mitchell was pushing her way through the crowd. Two of the guards started to move to prevent her from reaching us, but Mitchell stopped them.

In all the commotion, her hood had fallen down. Beautiful long crimson red hair came down around her. The same crimson red as my own hair. My eyes shot up to look at her face, staring back at me was my younger sister, Rias. Without another thought I was on my feet. My chair crashed to the floor behind me.

"Airis!" the girl called out. She collapsed into me and I wrapped my arms around her in a tight embrace.

"Rias!? How are you here? When did you get here? Are you okay?"

My questions were fired in rapid succession, with no time between them to let Rias respond. I turned quickly on my heel to face Hailey.

"Why didn't anyone tell me my sister was here— didn't you think that this would be something important!?"

Hailey's expression looked like she was caught by surprise as much as I was. Her hands came up quickly in defense.

"Hey, whoa—I—We had no clue she was your sister!" she turned to look at Mitchell for help, "Right Luke!? Tell her we didn't know!"

Mitchell frantically clambered up from his seat. His arms flailed about as he tried to point at Rias and Hailey.

"Listen, Commander Airis, we had no idea. Rias turned up at the old outpost with some others in a refugee caravan. We were packing the supplies and she mentioned that she had a background in alchemy. I asked her to help take down the alchemical workshop and set it back up, here at the camp."

Rias was still clinging on to me, and in between a few soft cries I could hear her muffled voice, "Luke and Hailey took me in. I didn't really know who to trust—So I never told anyone who I was, just my name."

My mind was racing. My first thoughts were ones of relief—but then I regained some focus and realized we were still in the middle of a command meeting.

Oh little sister, I was worried about you. But you're safe. Praise the Celestials.

Honestly, I had expected the worst. None of us knew if anyone who was left behind was safe or not. If Rias made it here, I wondered where our mother ended up...

I shook my head.

I relaxed my death gaze and got my mind back in the moment. The members of the assembly were all sitting here watching my family drama unfold. I could interrogate Mitchell and Hailey later.

With Rias still clutching to me, I turned us around so I'd be facing the meeting members. Rias was shorter than I was by a fair amount. Though I'm pretty sure she grew an inch or two since I last saw her. She was about the same height as Hailey now.

"My apologies for the drama. Consulates and Ministers, it is good to see you all again. Commander Brooks has briefed me on the status of the camp and your varied concerns and recommendations."

"To get this assembly back on track, I'll take over for a moment if you don't mind Airis."

I nodded, "All yours, Hailey."

Hailey clapped her hands together and everyone's attention snapped from Rias and I, to her.

"Okay. Listen up everybody! As of tonight, Commander Airis Vanixi is formally recognized by myself and the members of the Consulate as the acting High-Regent. Effective immediately she will be recognized as the High-Commander of the Vanixian Republic."

The Divisional soldiers stood at attention and saluted, arms tight across their chest. The abruptness of it startled Rias and she tightened her grip on me. I placed a hand on her head and held her close.

"At ease everyone, please. Let's keep the formalities limited for now so we can get through this expeditiously."

Hailey continued on, "Tomorrow morning all sectors are ordered to start breakdown procedures. As I said before, this is restricted information and you are only authorized to disclose details to those with proper clearances. With that said, Ministers and any Divisionals below the rank of Knight are clear to leave."

'Clear to leave', was just a polite way of saying 'you're not allowed to stay for the rest of the meeting'.

All members who were 'cleared to leave' left the command tent, leaving the Consulate members, Mitchell's scouting party, Hanna, and the few other soldiers I wasn't familiar with yet.

I shuffle-walked Rias to an empty seat near mine and sat her down. I sat down and looked at Julius, who was now giving me a stupid look.

Oh good, I can't wait to hear what sarcastic and dumb things he has to say about all of this.

With the remaining group seated and attentive, I began, "Here's the deal, we're all keen to stay alive. Nobody here is looking to sign up for a suicide mission like mounting an attack on Axio. We need to get reorganized and resupplied. Our aim right now is to get a permanent base of operations and get our footing back..."

I let my declaration settle for everyone, and then dropped the bomb, "Our goal for a permanent base, is the old Empire's port city of Tolin, in the south."

A rush of jumbled words came as everyone had something to say all at once. I raised my arm and the table quieted down.

"I'm aware of the stigma surrounding the city. I also acknowledge the concerns of moving into territory that fell under the Apocalypse. But we do not have another option. You've seen the state of things here. We cannot survive in the camp another month. There are no other options, there are no other places for us to go."

I brought out my map and laid it out on the table. I had scrawled a basic route to Tolin, detailing the mountain pass and the vast expanse of the Southern Plains.

"I doubt anyone here was around when Tolin fell, but it's not a simple history. Those of us who are alumni of VxA know the bare details, but my father had a special interest in the city."

Special interest indeed...

My father said that the fall of Tolin was the fulcrum that gave way to the fall of our Empire as we knew it, which ultimately led to the formation of the three republic Triumvirate government in Axio.

Rias had a pained look on her face at the mention of our father, but I continued on, "It is a nightmare-level kind of history. I know Tolin is large enough to house a group our size, and would have the infrastructure we need to get back into the fight fast."

"Nightmare status is putting it lightly, High-Regent." a woman spoke up. Mei Devins, one of Knight-Lieutenant Mitchell's team members. She continued, "We're talking about a city that fell in a single night. The population was decimated by monsters called 'Terror Demons', and that name doesn't give them the due they deserve."

"You're right. But with any luck in the forty-plus years since the city fell, those demons have moved on and an all-out assault isn't going to be necessary."

Julius cut in, "Even if there is some sort of monster presence in the city, we'll be prepared. When Tolin fell, humanity had barely a single skirmish with monsters. The Divisional Armies were created as a response to that threat. Airis and I propose the forming of a vanguard party with our best people. With the addition of supportive parties we can form a coalition force and take on whatever horrors may face us."

I gave Hailey a nod and she stood, "I'm ordering the disbandment of scouting parties seven and twelve. Mei and Luke of scouting party seven, and Alcotts and Jameson of scouting party twelve will be redeployed to the Vanguard team. Along with myself, High-Protector Julius, and High-Commander Airis."

Devins, Alcotts and Jameson had been introduced to Julius and I before the meeting started.

Crusader Mei Devins was a seasoned veteran. A half-elven oddity, her father was a citizen of the Empire, her mother was an *Aestori*, a race of elves that lived within the Empire whose name translated to Starfallen. Although easily over one-hundred years old, she was youthful in appearance. I found myself distracted by her beauty more than once. Her porcelain skin and silky violet hair framed a slender face and long ears in a way that made her look like a sculptured masterpiece.

Crusader Alistaire Alcotts was very personable. He greeted both of us with enthusiasm. He looked young, in his early twenties, with a mess of reddish-orange hair on his head. His features were soft, and unmistakably foreign. The most striking of which were his eyes, I couldn't help but be smitten with them: green on the right, red to the left.

His presence was a quandary to be sure, but if Hanna and Hailey trusted him then so would I.

Crusader Soren Jameson's personality was the polar opposite of Alcotts. He was incredibly shy and reserved, Alcotts did most of the talking for him. He looked younger than his partner, but the way he carried himself gave an air of maturity. His hair was styled short around the front and sides, coming together into a long tail in the back.

Julius' took the next turn to speak, "I will take the role of Initiator, as I'm the only one in the party with a guardian specialty. Airis will take on the Operator role, and uniquely as a hybrid specialization she will assist Hailey in healing, while also keeping her protected with some newly acquired blade skills."

He continued, "Luke will be our Field Monitor, he's the only one with a rogue specialization that can track enemy movements and watch for traps or ambushes. Alcotts and Jameson, you are both with me. As you're both Warriors, you will switch out with each other during combat to keep your cycle times low. If anything happens to take us by surprise we'll always have one of you ready to resolve it."

Both warriors gave Julius an odd look.

"What about that isn't clear? Address it now so we don't have misunderstandings later." Julius said bluntly.

They both sat there, silently, as their faces turned more red.

Alcotts was the one to speak up, "I don't believe either of us have heard the term 'switch out'. Would you explain that, High-Protector?"

Jameson nodded his head in agreement with his partner.

Since neither of them were officers, they wouldn't have attended VxA. It makes sense they maybe wouldn't be familiar with the terms... But they have to had someone managing combat cycles on their previous team.

Julius had already started explaining the overall concept to them before I had a chance to ask about their last party.

"I understand. During combat, your stamina will decrease the longer you stay engaged with an enemy. That is referred to as a combat cycle. Typically once your stamina is past a certain point you will begin to suffer short-lived penalties. If it hits zero, you'll start to gain long-term fatigue. And if you continue fighting after you've starting stacking fatigue effects, you may fall unconscious... or worse."

Julius tapped his wrist and his rune lit up, the space above the table filled with aetheric mist. A visual depiction of a stamina bar was projected onto the mist.

"Anyone with an OVERSIGHT skill, like Airis," he pointed a finger at me, "can see a party member's stamina gauge. She can watch these during combat and could call out for members to switch places in a fight."

He placed his finger over the rune and the mists dispersed.

"Cycles prevent either of you from suffering any penalties, and it will also ensure that one of you is always un-engaged to address any unexpected issues. Make sense?"

Both Jameson and Alcotts nodded. Alcotts leaned into Jameson and whispered something in his ear. The timid warriors eyes lit up and he let out an 'ahhhh'.

As I suspected, they had been doing this already but didn't understand Julius' use of phrase. I allowed the brief doubt in Hanna's party forming abilities to fade away.

Julius continued his assignments review. "Lastly, Devins. As a ranger specialty you're going to be responsible for keeping pressure on targets Luke calls out. As I understand from Hailey, you have an Eagle companion, correct?"

Devins stepped into view from a place in the back of the room.

"That is correct. Her name is Valiance, she's a Ebonfeather Eagle. She has a STEALTH skill, as well as a MARK TARGET passive ability."

Woah, that's one special companion.

Now I was curious. I missed whatever conversation Julius may have had with Hailey about that. I interrupted Julius before he could continue ahead,

"An Ebonfeather Eagle? That's incredible. Would you mind telling me how you managed to tame such a rare animal?"

The elven ranger shook her head.

"I did not tame her. She is my *PAERIR*. A soulmate from the day we were brought forth to this world. In the Starfall Forest I was raised as a *SYLVAE CAETOS*. A Forest Guardian. This is quite common."

Julius and I both exchanged looks.

Was he impressed?

His normal stoneface demeanor had been shaken a little, his eyes had widened slightly.

"That's... quite something. Thank you." I set my whole attention to Julius, "Is there anything else you wanted to add, or are we all set?"

"I think we're all set. The last thing is," Julius pointed at the other soldiers at the table, "You will get party assignments tonight after I finish unit inspections."

Hailey pointed at Hanna, "Hanna, you're going to be the acting outpost commander once we get a foothold at Tolin. I trust you to keep things orderly while we're busy."

Hanna gave a salute and a head bow in response.

I tapped my rune and brought up a party interface and added my new party members.

Julius had gotten the team recommendations from Mitchell while they were preparing our tent earlier. I trusted his judgment, we're going to succeed at this.

Hailey dismissed everyone and they filed out of the command tent.

Rias had fallen asleep during our meeting. I gently shook her awake, and arm-in-arm with my sleepy eyed sister I let Julius lead us to our tent.

It wasn't as big as the command tent, but it was noticeably larger than the other tents in the camp. It stood next to two other tents of equal size, Hailey's and then Mitchell and Hanna's.

I tucked Rias into my bed under a pile of warm blankets, she was back to sleep in seconds.

"Don't think just because you're giving up your bed to your sister that you get to steal my bed away from me." Julius joked dryly, his voice low, almost a whisper.

"You'd force your High-Regent to sleep out in the cold?"

"I would do exactly that."

"Ruuude." I returned in a melodramatic way, "Well it doesn't matter anyway. I wasn't planning to kick you from your bed. Rias turns into an ice block when she sleeps, and I radiate heat like an over-stoked hearth. We're a match made by the Celestials. So, you'll get your bed all to yourself just like you wanted."

"Fantastic," Julius wore his trademark smirk wide across his face, "I won't have to worry about coming back and finding out I'm out of a bed to sleep in." His smirk dropped and was replaced with his other trademark face, seriousness, "I'll be out inspecting the Divisionals and coordinating the party formations tonight. Don't wait up for me."

"Take it easy on them, Julius. It's been a rough two weeks for everyone. Don't get bent out of shape if their beds aren't made with tight corner sheets."

"You got it, High-Regent."

A deep drawn-out yawn escaped me.

I am going to collapse in this bed and sleep forever. Today has been the longest day imaginable. Julius almost died...

As thoughts of sleep tip-toed through my mind, Hailey's head poked in through the tent and any chances of getting to bed were swept away.

"Oh! Good, you're not sleeping yet. Come out here, I have something for you."

I stepped outside slowly, each step heavy with a paralytic nervousness.

She handed me a glass bottle and pleaded, "Come on, have a drink with me."

I looked down at the bottle in my hands. It was semi-opaque, but I could make out the label and pinkish color of the liquid inside. It was a brand of sweet rosé from Axio, Starfury Rubrum Reserve. It was my favorite kind, and only available in the winter from a few merchants.

A wave of emotions crashed down on me. After the day we'd been through I was barely hanging on. A swell of tears threatened to break through my facade.

Hailey inched closer as she waited for a response. Anxiety wriggled its way into my nerves. I didn't know what to say.

I want to spend time with her, but being near her makes me anxious.

"I know you've had a rough day. A rough few weeks, even... So I brought you your favorite wine." Her smile beamed up at me.

My heart skipped.

She knew it was my favorite wine?

Hailey grabbed my hand and my heart started racing.

She led me back to her tent—rather, what I thought was her tent. As I was dragged in behind her, we were met by a very surprised Mitchell and Hanna.

"Look who I found!" Hailey sang out.

Hanna let out a little yelp at the sudden intrusion. "Hailey! What are you doing? It's late and we're exhausted."

"We're drinking, to celebrate Airis' return from the dead..." She paused, tapping her chin in thought, "annnnd the reunion of two sisters, and to... the new High-Regent!"

Her words were drawn out and a little slurred.

"I get the feeling that you may have started celebrating before us." Mitchell let out a chuckle.

Hailey shushed Mitchell and plopped herself down on the edge of the bed. She pulled out two more bottles from a satchel, hidden under her cloak.

When did Hailey become so rebellious?

I let out a nervous laugh and took a drink from my bottle. The sparkling wine's fruity aroma was captivating. A perfect distraction to calm my nerves.

"Have I ever told you about the day Airis and I met?" Hailey was leaning towards Mitchell, but looking at Hanna.

Mitchell's reply was soft, like the tone you'd take with a child, "Often. But we'd never tire of it, Hailey."

"Good!" Hailey shot up energetically, "Because it's my favorite story. But I want Airis to tell it this time!" She flopped back onto the bed. Smiling wildly at me, she patted her hand down next to her.

What in the Aether? When did I get demoted to story teller?

I took another swig out of my bottle and settled down next to Hailey.

"Sooo... Where to start?"

"Tell them about the coin thing!"

My hand came to rest against my face.

The coin thing. Oh by the Celestials I had forgotten that I had done that.

Awkwardly I started, "I had just been told my class assignment after aptitude testing. The Magister led me to an empty classroom and told me to take a seat, but I didn't know where I wanted to sit."

I shook my head in shame and laughed, "So a few minutes pass by and another girl is dropped off at the classroom." I glanced over to Hailey, who was grinning ear to ear. "I asked her if she wanted to take a chance on where we'd sit."

I pulled my coin out from my pocket.

Hailey burst out an excited squeal, "That's the coin! Oh wow, I didn't expect you to have it with you."

Her attention was captivated by the coin.

"I told her that we could flip a coin, we'd each call a side, and whoever's side came up got to pick where we sat. I called tails—"

"But I wanted tails! So she let me have tails."

"And I let Hailey have tails."

I flipped my coin up into the air. The dull lantern light in the tent didn't give it much of a sparkle, and it fell back to my hand unceremoniously. I quickly capped the back of my hand with my other.

My three drinking companions watched as I pulled my hand back.

"And I won!" Hailey exclaimed as the crimson-red wings of a phoenix glinted lightly.

"Hailey chose the two front and center seats... And we had to deal with being picked on by the Magister for the rest of the year."

"I apologized everyday, I felt so bad. It was a nightmare. That Magister did not like us at all!"

"Her excuse was that she was so excited to learn about Magick that she didn't want to miss a thing."

Hanna and Mitchell broke out into light laughter while Hailey pouted.

"I *was* excited about Magick..."

We traded off telling stories of our time at VxA together. I finished off my bottle of Starfury and was presented with a second bottle, from Hailey's secret cloak stash.

FIVE

AWAKE. UUUUUGH. AM I AWAKE ALREADY?

I tightened my eyelids as my mind stirred.

I refuse to wake up on my own. I'm going to sleep until someone drags me from this bed—

Ahhh! What was that!?

Something in my bed was wriggling wildly next to me. My eyes shot open wide.

A curly mess of red hair filled my vision.

Oh. It's just Rias.

I was in a curled position, lying on my left side. My sister was sprawled out next to me, squirming against a pillow.

I gently swept her invasive strands of hair away from my face and closed my eyes. Just as I was falling back to sleep—I was jarred back awake.

A new sensation from behind caused my body to shudder. Something was intertwining itself around my legs. I was unable to twist around to see who—or what—was behind me, so I slowly craned my neck around. Just within my periphery, an arm lazily moved its way up my side, coming to rest across my chest.

A small hand clenched tightly to my shirt, coming dangerously close to grabbing more than just cloth...

A soft mumbly voice came from the same side as the arm.

"Mmmm... Is it morning already, Airis?"

After freeing my legs I slowly twisted around, as to not disturb Rias, and found myself face to face with another mess of red hair. Hailey's cherry-red hair, to be precise.

Okay, what!? What in the name of the Celestials is happening??

Hailey looked at me sleepily, her eyes barely cracked open.

"Whaaa...?" she mumbled.

The events of last night drifted into thought, and although they were a bit hazy, I definitely remembered Hailey walking me back to my tent... And staying, apparently, as I couldn't recall her leaving.

Hailey snuggled her face into my neck and wrapped her arm back around me. Her leg coiled its way around my own.

Out of my control, a weak 'eep' escaped my lips. My face was hot and my chest felt like it would burst at any minute.

"Mmm... Go back to sleep, it's too early..."

Hailey and I were close when we attended the Academy together. We had shared a dormitory room, and I used to convince her to stay up until absurd hours of the night with me. We'd study until we were so exhausted that eventually we'd end up falling asleep together, just like this.

What I never told anyone though, was that I just wanted her to sleep in the same bed as me because I had a major crush on her... A decade later and it still looks like nothings changed.

Another flash of last nights events stirred in my mind. Realization flooded in.

Hailey had walked me back to my tent. Before heading back to her own, she gave me a hug. But I didn't want to let her go... And...

Oh Celestials...

I asked her to stay the night with me, like we used to.

Rias tossed over in her sleep and now had her head pressed up against my back, trapping me in place. Exhausted and facing new levels of drama if I tried to escape, I chose to close my eyes and try to get back to sleep.

Get ahold of yourself, Airis.

I was woken up by a finger repeatedly poking my face. I cracked one eye open.

Julius was staring down at me. His eyes drifted to my right, then my left, then returned to me. I wasn't sure what kind of look was on his face... Ah—no, I had it. This was concentrated confusion, but with a hint of smugness.

A brand new original Julius expression.

"Not one word. I will kill you." I whispered sharply up to him.

"I have... just so many questions."

Hailey shifted in bed, "Mmmmm—oh, hey Julius." She turned her body back towards mine and buried her face against my back, "Five more minutes..."

"Why didn't you tell me?" Julius asked.

"Tell you what?" I hissed.

"That you two were a thing."

I felt my face flush with heat, "We aren't—I don't— She's—" I stammered, unable to come up with anything cohesive, "C-Can we not have this conversation right now!?"

Julius started to speak but broke off and turned around. I heard someone stepping into our tent. Mitchell came into view, his face was pale.

"Julius, Commander Airis, have you seen Hailey? I checked her tent this morning but she was..." His voice trembled slightly with panic, but it slowly drifted off as he looked from Julius, to me, to Hailey. He stood there silently as he tried to comprehend the scene.

"Good morning, Luke. As it turns out, I have seen Hailey." Julius grabbed him by the shoulders and led him back out of the tent, "Come on, let's go grab some breakfast."

I'm not going to catch a break with this at all.

Luke's entrance had woken up Hailey. She started laughing hysterically, which in turn, woke up my sister.

Rias rubbed her eyes and let out a yawn. She stared blankly at the wriggling mass of blankets Hailey having a giggle fit underneath.

"Hmm... Hailey?" Rias mumbled, barely audible, as she looked at me, "Did she sleep in our bed last night? What is so funny?"

I refused to answer. My embarrassment level had reached a new peak. I reached for a sheet to hide my own self under, but Hailey had managed to hog them all.

Hailey was now having trouble catching her breath in the midst of her laugh attack, "It's just that—he was probably so worried! And then he comes in here... ahaha!"

Her laughter renewed its ferocity and she was left unable to form coherent words. Rias continued to stare blankly at me, waiting for an explanation.

I covered my bright-red face with both hands and refused to give her an answer.

"Sis, are you okay?"

I shook my head and slowly crept out of bed, intent to track down my clothes.

After Hailey had calmed down, she stuck her face out of the tent and got a guard to grab her two fresh uniforms.

She held out one of the uniforms, complete with a Commander's insignia, for me to take. As I took it, our eyes met.

"H-hey, about last night, and this morning, I..." my eyes darted around the room

She leaned in close and her eyes sparkled, "Yeeeah?"

You can't tell her. You can't tell her. You can't tell her. Don't say anything stupid, Airis.

My heart was racing again.

"I-I, umm... wanted to say thank you, for the wine."

"Anytime!"

Once we had finished getting changed, she grabbed onto Rias and I, dragging us from the tent.

We ended up at the command tent, where Julius, Mitchell, and Hanna were already eating. I sat down a few chairs away from Julius.

I am not getting baited into any of his nonsense this morning.

Rias and Hailey sat on either side of me.

Great, from the bed to the breakfast table.

Mitchell shifted uncomfortably in his seat as he shoveled food into his mouth.

Hanna and Hailey left together after breakfast to get status updates from all the camp's sectional leaders. Which left Mitchell, Rias, Julius, and I to figure out where we could be helpful. Rias was the first one to offer up a genuinely good idea to begin our day

"I've been tinkering with a new invention for the last few days with Dori's help. I asked her to pair an action class Sonic enchantment and a combat class Aether enchantment to enhance some small handheld runes. If you channel a small amount of magick to it, it will let you connect to any of the other runes over a far distance. In theory, you can talk into it and it will transfer your voice on the other end. She should have them done, would you mind going with me to see her?"

"Magic runes that allow you to speak over long distances? Sounds like some artificer fiction to me, Rias. But of course I'll go with you." I gave Julius a wave, "Byeee. You boys are on your own this morning."

And we left before they could protest.

The camp was in a frenzy. Tents were being torn down, supplies boxed up, and wagons loaded. It was quite a sight to see how organized the whole process was being handled. I had expected there to be a little more disorder.

The blacksmith's tent was a few minutes walk from where the command tent was positioned. I looked over at Rias, who was scampering ahead of me.

"Hey, Rias. Hold up a second!"

She skipped forwards and spun around. "Of course! Are you feeling okay? You were acting weird this morning."

Gah!

"I'm feeling just fine, thank you. I wanted to talk to you about how you ended up at the camp with Luke and Hailey. I thought you were returning to your school?"

"Oh, well I was."

I waited for her to keep going. I leaned my head towards her and raised my eyebrows.

"But what happened? How did you wind up here? Don't get me wrong, I'm relieved you're okay. And I'm happy you're safe. But..."

"But what?"

But I'm worried I'm about to take you with me into a battleground.

I shook my head.

"Doesn't matter I guess," I grabbed her side and pulled her in for a hug, "knowing you're safe is the important thing."

Rias returned my embrace and we scuttled forward.

"I don't know how we ended up here really. After I got to Dori's schoolhouse, she had us pack everything up and we left the city that night."

Of course, Dörien the artificer was Rias' teacher. A lock lifted and the gears in my brain started to spin freely.

As we passed through the camp I got more than my fair share of greetings and salutes. Apparently the news had made its way around the camp that Hailey and the Consulate had appointed me as the acting High-Regent.

Rias and I arrived at where the blacksmith's tent had been, but found only a large wagon packed to the maximum with crates and soot covered stones.

"You think your runes got packed up in those crates?"

"Maybe... I hope not."

Dörien's head popped up from behind one of the crates on the wagon, calling out to Rias.

"Oi! Lil' tinkerer, over 'ere."

"Dori! Hey! Did you get a chance to finish that rune project? I wanted to show it off to Airis."

"Aye, got 'em right 'ere."

She dug out a handful of coin sized runes from a rucksack near her feet and handed them down to Rias. "Gettin' yer' points in wit' the new High-Commander are ye' lil' tinkerer?"

"I don't have to worry about that, Dori," Rias let out a chuckle and then grabbed me in a side hug, "Airis is my big sister."

Dörien stared intensely at us, her eyes darted back and forth between Rias and me. "Aye... Guess ye' could see a resemblance."

We left Dörien to get back to her tasks. Rias handed me one of the runes.

"Here, take one. Place it just in front of your ear and give it a light tap. It should stay in place once activated."

I looked it over in my hand. It was a small unassuming runestone with elaborate carvings. "Have you decided what you're going to name this project of yours, little sister?"

"I've been calling them 'Communirunes' for now. Got a better idea?"

I let out a light sigh, followed by a groan.

Rias gave me a great big smile, "So it's a perfect name, then. Thanks sis!"

LOOTABLES

Item	Attributes	Description
COMMUNIRUNE	-	A small intricate rune. Enchanted with Sonic and Aether magick. Allows for long distance communication.

I did as Rias explained and tapped the rune while near my ear. The rune gave me a harmless static shock when it energized, but it caused me to jump a little bit. I let out a yelp by reflex.

"Eeek!"

"Oh sorry! I forgot to mention that they should channel magicka from you to work. It's a negligible amount though, even someone without an affinity for Aether can use them."

I gave Rias a look of mock disappointment.

"Come ooon. I bet it didn't even hurt! Let's test them out. Just stay here, I'll stand over there and you'll see how awesome these are."

Rias ran a fair distance away. She was close enough that I could still see her, but there was no way I'd be able to hear her say anything. I'm not sure I'd even be able to hear her well if she was yelling.

The faint hum of magickal energy filled my ears, followed by the crystal clear voice of my sister, "Heeey Airis, can you hear me?"

"Yeah, Sis. I can hear you."

"Awesome!"

"So, how do these things work? I know once you've energized them they're on. But I didn't sense any magickal energy until you started talking to me."

"Dori said she enchanted them to be intent based. Basically, if you subconsciously think about who you want to be able to hear you, your rune should transmit to theirs."

I can't believe these little runes could be so complex. That dwarf really knows her stuff.

I rejoined Rias and we started heading back to the command tent. It was past noon now, and I wanted to get our party together to make sure these runes worked for everyone.

We arrived—but the command tent was already being taken down. A quick scan around nearby and we found the members of my party gathered together close by. Julius spotted me at the same time and waved us over.

I shoved a rune into his palm, "Here, stick this to your face."

He gave me a blank stare but, after seeing the rune I had placed near my ear, he placed the rune near his and gave it a tap. His posture tightened slightly and the blank look narrowed sharply to a piercing gaze.

In a voice rich in sarcasm, dramatically I clutched my hand to my chest, "Oh, did I forget to mention that it would give you a little jolt? I'm so sorry."

That's what you get for messing with me this morning!

I handed out runes to the rest of the party, giving a second one to Mitchell to give to Hanna later. Rias explained how they worked to the whole team.

When everyone had settled back down I tapped my wrist rune and brought up a party visual. I added the members to our party, and assigned the designated roles. It wouldn't be long before we'd be heading out.

It should be about that time any minute. The camp is pretty much packed up and wagons have already started to head out of the clearing.

Hanna approached with a small group of soldiers with her. I recognized a few of them from the remainder of Luke's scouting party yesterday. They must have been assigned under Hanna's party last night.

Hanna saluted Hailey and I, her right arm snapping into place across her chest with precision.

"Camp breakdown is completed, Commanders. I've given orders for all sectors to depart. They're underway as we speak."

I returned her salute, "Thanks, Hanna. At ease. Mitchell has something for you. I would appreciate it if you would take it and see Rias, she'll explain how to use it."

"I'll see them right away." She started to walk away but paused mid step and turned back, "Hey Commander, I was wondering something. Why don't you call Luke by his given name, but you call me by mine?"

I gave her a blank look, "Hmmm..." I tapped my chin with my left index finger.

Why don't I call Mitchell by his given name?

I shrugged, "If I had to guess, It's because when we met, he introduced himself as 'Knight-Lieutenant Mitchell'. But when you and I met, you were just 'Hanna'. I didn't really notice I was doing that."

She let out a huge sigh, "Oh, okay! We were worried you didn't like him."

Mitchell had walked over during our conversation, and his face was completely red again.

Poor guy couldn't catch a break today. Hanna patted him on the shoulder, "Luke, good news! The commander doesn't hate you!"

I looked at the now ruby red face of my party member, "Would you like it if I called you Luke? If so, I have no problem if that's what you'd prefer."

"Y—you really don't have to, Commander. It's not a big deal. Really." He stammered.

"Well it's settled then, Luke. Now, if you would please take Hanna to see Rias and get her all set I'd appreciate it."

"Of course, Commander! I'll get her all caught up."

Hailey had been watching our exchange and let out a laugh. She followed after Luke and Hanna.

I packed up the rest of my gear and helped Julius load our equipment onto our horses.

When the three returned from getting Hanna's Communirune setup, we all rode together to the front of the marching army.

The mountain pass was still quite a few hours away. And Tolin was a two day ride from the outpost, but with this many soldiers on foot it could easily take double or triple that.

It would give me plenty of time to think.

I pulled my coin from my pocket, and Julius and I started calling sides for who would decide on potential battle plans.

We made camp at the mountain summit and I was planning to settle in for bed as soon as possible.

I was exhausted from a day of riding. Everyone else seemed to have the same feelings too, because after dinner they practically crawled into their tents.

Julius, Rias, and I had agreed to share a tent again. He had offered to get his own tent, of course. But I hadn't spent a night away from Julius in the last few weeks, and his presence had become a sort of calming coping mechanism for me to be able to get to sleep. I responded to his suggestion with a piercing glare and he retracted the offer.

I disrobed unceremoniously and flopped into bed, Rias was already fast asleep by the time I had gotten back from dinner. My head hit the pillow and I closed my eyes. I had almost drifted off to sleep, when I heard Hailey's voice from the entryway.

"Airis, are you still awake?" "

Just a few words and I was out of rhythm.

I lifted myself up, clutching a sheet close to my body, "Yeah. I'm up. Did you need something, Hails?"

I could hear her boots scrape against the dirt as she kicked her foot around.

"I completely forgot to have someone make me up a tent... And so I'm kinda without a place to sleep—"

"—You want to sleep here!?"

"Is that okay?"

"I—We just have the two beds so you'd..."

Have to sleep with me...

I was so nervous I couldn't even bring myself to even say the words. She had stepped into the tent and was now hovering above me in bed.

She bent down and softly whispered into my ear, "It's not like I haven't slept with you before, Airis."

I swallowed hard and tried to keep my face from flooding with embarrassment.

"You have to watch your phrasing!"

She giggled and dramatically placed a hand over her mouth, "Whaaat? Did I say something wrong?"

Hailey spent a moment taking off her gear. She glanced over towards Julius, who was already asleep.

Or at least pretending to be, I'm sure I'll hear about this in the morning. I can hear his smugness already.

She stripped down into her smallclothes and slipped in under the sheets. Her soft breath slowed in pace.

No matter how hard I tried I couldn't settle myself down.

After I was certain she was asleep, I carefully adjusted in bed so that I was facing her. The bed sheet clung close to her chest. Rising and falling with each breath.

I synchronized my own breathing with hers.

In... Out... In... Out... She's so beautiful—Gaaah!

I mentally slapped myself and focused on the slow and steady breathing until my eyelids grew heavy and I finally fell asleep.

SIX

THE NEXT FOUR DAYS WERE A STEADY PACED boring routine. Each day was the same; wake up at an hour that made me cry, eat breakfast, break down camp, ride along the marching army for about eight hours, set up camp, eat dinner, and then go to sleep.

Our journey up the mountain pass was mostly uneventful. A few soldiers ended up with minor scrapes and bruises after losing their footing on the poorly kept roadway, nothing our healers couldn't cure.

Weathering over the last few decades had left the trail in a poor state. Squared stones were fit together in a diagonally crossing pattern, though now the stones were loose and had years of erosion. Powerful storms had washed more than a few feet of the road away in places.

The pace of the convoy was slowed by a day overall as we traveled through the pass. We had to stop to make repairs on more than a few broken wagon wheels.

I praised the Celestials when I rounded the final bend before we began our descent. I was sure we were blessed to not have lost a single soul.

On top of that we didn't lose any supplies.

In another few days, we'd arrive at our destination.

The long trip was actually an advantage for our new party. I thought so, at least.

I was able to have some relaxed conversations with Alistaire and Soren. The second night had been tense as Julius decided he wanted to run drills and practice team formations. Awkwardly, we squared up against Hanna's team—and promptly got our asses handed to us.

But after a night of drinking and joking around, the two took to Julius and started working well as a team.

Mei and Luke had a unique synergy, through a series of shorthand calls over their Communirunes they became the perfect overwatch team.

To the detriment of my own anxiety, Hailey had been spending most of her time with me. I was happy for the attention, even if I was nervous every waking minute now. And it allowed Luke and Hanna to open up to me.

The two of them were long time childhood friends of Hailey's. We would stay up late telling old stories and discussing new strategies.

Honestly, after traveling with them for a week, I felt like they were my old friends too.

Julius had taken Alistaire and Soren under his wing, so far as to manage getting another bed requisitioned in their tent for himself.

This left Rias and I on our own. She took over his bed, though she had it moved closer to mine, claiming concerns over not being able to sleep unless I was close by. That development didn't trouble me...

What was alarming, was when Hailey asked if she could share the tent with us. I had no valid reason to give against the idea—not to mention that I kind of liked the thought of her sharing a space with me again, like out VxA days.

And so we traded one tent-mate for another.

On the final night before we'd arrive at Tolin, Hailey stopped me before we settled down for the night.

"Can I steal you away for a bit? I want to talk about something... In private." Her voice was hushed, to avoid anyone from overhearing.

"O-of course!"

She gave me a look of relief, and grabbed her staff. I glanced over at my sword, lying near my bed in its scabbard, but she shook her head to indicate I wouldn't need it.

Trusting her, I followed after her and we looked for a quiet spot away from camp. Once we were safely tucked away behind a rocky outcrop, she held her staff out.

"This was a gift from my mother."

The staff that she carried with her was unassuming. It was made from an ebony bough that had a strange interlocking grain. At the centerpiece, a small golden ovate jewel was clasped by a lune-shaped gnarl in the wood.

"I remember when you got it during our valediction ceremony—but I thought that your father gave it to you?"

She smiled, "He did. But, it was my mother's... and it was her mother's before that. This staff is a family secret of sorts. At least, that's what my father told me."

Her expression was hard to read. I knew she wanted to talk to me about something that was personal.

Now isn't the time to hesitate! I need to be here for her.

I stepped in close and took her free hand. I wanted to say something to reassure her, to comfort her. She looked up at me, and I was lost in her rosy-pink eyes twinkling under the starlight. I was sinking deep into a well of emotions and nothing I could think of seemed adequate enough—so I said nothing and just squeezed her hand tightly.

Her face softened and she squeezed my hand back.

"My mother passed away when I was really young. I don't remember her all that well. Whatever stories she may have told me as a child—anything to do with this staff, were lost with her. However, my father told me one thing. That my grandmother was a priestess. She belonged to a sect of the Empire's upper echelon, called the Order of the Light."

I strained my mind, reaching deep into my memories, trying to recall if I had ever heard of such a group... My family history was intertwined with the Church of the Consecrated Light, the founding doctrine of the Empire—which was commonly referenced as The Empire of the Light.

But an Order of the Light..?

If that order did exist, it may be lost to time.

Hailey must have sensed that I had drawn a blank, and kept on speaking.

"Anyway, what I really wanted to talk to you about is..." She trailed off, looking lost in thought.

I gave her hand another squeeze.

"You can tell me anything, Hails."

She sighed, letting her shoulders drop, "I've always been able to easily channel magick through my staff. It's not like those awful training staves back at the Academy. I've never had any feedback issues like with those shoddy focus crystals... That is, until recently... it's not normal. Something about it feels off."

"When did it start happening?"

"The day that we fled Axio..."

She looked down at her staff and slipped her hand from mine. Her slender fingers ran across the darkwood near the centerpiece.

"Do you mind if I show you what I mean?"

I nodded.

Taking my hand, she placed it over the jewel at the staff's head. She closed her eyes and I felt a pressure change in the air as she channeled magick through the crystal.

A short double-beating pulse emanated from the jewel, almost like a heartbeat. It was calming. The rhythmic sensation gave me a reassuring feeling, that of a closeness to a loved one. Like resting your head on their chest as their heart pounded—At least until the fourth beat, when a sharp pain jolted through my arm.

I gasped and pulled my hand back.

"What in the Aether was that!?"

"T-that's what I was talking about! It's not normal spell feedback. I don't think this is just some heirloom... I had hoped you knew about it from—Waaah?"

The pale-golden jewel began to shine erratically.

Like a bird spreading its wings before taking flight, ethereal feathers sprang into existence around the staff's head. They shimmered as if they were alive with flame.

The jewel now radiated a reddish-orange that pulsed in cadence with a soft feminine voice that spoke, seemingly, from inside my own head.

"So, the priestess has finally brought me to the Empress."

Hailey flinched at the same time as the voice spoke. She flailed around, looking out into the darkness around us.

"Who said that? Who's out there!?"

The jewel flashed in the same fashion as before in response, but flared brightly as it finished.

"I am not out there. I'm in here."

We both stared at the jewel in shock.

I wasn't sure what to make of this turn of events: Hailey was having troubles with her staff, and now all of a sudden we're hearing a disembodied voice coming from it.

"Airis, why is my focus crystal talking to me? And why does it sound like it's in my own head!?"

"I heard it too, Hails, but I don't have an answer."

"The touch of the Empress woke me, though only for a short while. I am nearing the cycle of my rebirth, but it is not time yet."

"..."

Hailey remained silent, her mouth agape. Her eyes pleaded with me for help.

"What are you?"

"I am Ignicorus."

"And you are... the staff?"

"I am not the staff."

"..."

Well, at least it wasn't some kind of bewitched sentient object. But that didn't help narrow down what we were dealing with. I once again wracked my mind for anything I may have learned about something named Ignicorus...

Ignicorus... Why did that sound familiar?—OH!

A distant memory flooded back to the center of my mind.

IGNI was the elven glyph for fire, and CORUS was the glyph for blaze. Translated literally, it would mean 'blaze of fire', but in the common tongue, it would be spoken as Flameblaze.

Which also happened to be the Divine figure at the head of the Church of the Consecrated Light...

"Are you telling us that you're Flameblaze, the Phoenix God!?" I asked incredulously.

"It's nice to hear that I haven't been completely forgotten."

Hailey looked at me with a puzzled expression and I explained as best I could.

"It's a story my mother used to read to me before bed, *Flameblaze and the Embers of Redemption*. I thought it was just a children's story back then. But I stumbled across the book a few years ago and realized it was actually a lengthy nonfiction about the Empire's Phoenix God."

In truth, the book was a religious text that was brought to Axio when the refugees fled during the Empire's fall after the Apocalypse. A number of noble Houses still practiced the Church's doctrine as closely as they could. My parents weren't as devout as some, but our House did consider itself to be of the Church.

I looked back at the pulsating gemstone held in the staff. I finally realized why it looked so strange to me. It wasn't shaped like any ornately cut gem that would be used as a focus crystal—it was entirely egg shaped.

I pointed at the egg.

"That, is the regenerating vessel of the Phoenix God of the Church of the Consecrated Light."

The golden egg's light dimmed in intensity for a moment before flickering brightly.

Instinctively, I reached my hand out but stopped short of grasping the staff when the light came back.

"I am waning... I must return to my torporous state—but I will rise soon. You must prepare for my arrival, Priestess of the Light."

The shining glow began to dull, though the flame-like glowing feathers remained.

Hailey's expression was the same bewildered one as it was a moment ago. She looked from me, to her staff, and back to me.

"What!?"

We returned to our tent after an unsatisfactory attempt to come to terms with what had just happened. Hailey mumbled something about how her head hurt before crawling into bed.

I stared at the canvas ceiling above me for a while, my mind raced with questions. Three thoughts swirled around my head.

What did it mean by 'prepare for my arrival'?
Why did it call me 'Empress'?
Would Julius believe us if we told him?

The morning sun peeked over the horizon, and the red-clay tile roofs of Tolin could be seen in the distance peeking over the city's massive walls. While the city may have once been a large seaport, it was also pushing the frontiers of the Empire's boundaries. The defensive capabilities of the city were second-rate to none. Tolin wasn't as sprawling as Axio, but it had a certain grandness to it that tricked the eye to believe it was larger than it really was.

The buildings and walls were built of pinkish-white volcanic rock called *Vyae*. A large castle-tower with three adjoined turrets loomed over the market district, and a red-stone citadel shadowed the buildings in the western section of the city.

I took a few deep breaths to steady myself. With me, I had an army large enough to easily take the city; even if we encountered resistance. My harebrained plan, cooked up in a small village tavern, to conquer the city was almost coming to fruition.

Only the so-called Terror Demons and a horde of monsters might be in our way.

That was all.

As we approached, the state of the city and the damage it had suffered became more apparent. I borrowed Julius' binoculars to get a better view of the external walls.

The gates of Tolin were splintered open. Scorched earth from a powerful magick explosion still marred the ground. The city walls were covered by decaying makeshift fortifications of raw timber.

The city had been made ready for a siege—A siege that ended before it even started.

Historical journals said that the demonic hordes materialized out of the Aethermist and devastated the city's defenders. Tolin fell in a single night.

Our blessings endured, because the rolling plains and fields leading to the city seemed to be deserted.

The bulk of our convoy stopped to make camp at a rundown farm about a mile from the city gates. I saw Julius pass by me, he was helping some Divisionals carry spiked barricades towards the front of camp.

A small regiment of Divisionals continued on the road with more barricades. They would be creating a checkpoint and guard post closer to the city gates. A number of windmills dotted the fields, and would make for a great makeshift spotting tower.

Before sundown, we had a fully functioning outpost. Engineers were leading teams to dig out the earthworks around the camp, they would be finished before morning.

Most of the supplies and equipment from the forest encampment remained packed away in crates. We would make a determination on breaking those down once we understood our position better.

Hailey and I dispatched scouting parties. A total of seven teams. Four teams would head through the gates and stealthily move around the city. Three teams would remain outside and survey the perimeter walls for weak spots or alternative ways inside.

Alistaire and Soren showed up just as we sent out the last team.

"Commanders, the command tent is all ready. Paladin Vynn is waiting for you there, she asked us to find you both."

Hailey clapped her hands.

"Great! I can hand over responsibility for this camp off to Hanna," she turned to me and placed her hands across her stomach, "then we can track down something to eat!"

We took off towards the center of camp, but I turned back to address the two boys.

"Will you two be joining us for dinner, or are you doing your own thing tonight?"

"We'll catch up with you two in a moment. Soren and I are going to get a tent claimed before all the good ones are gone." Alistaire gave me a toothy grin.

I caught up with Hailey and we walked to the command tent together. Hanna was waiting for us inside, the two of them started to go over camp preparation, section statuses, and other incredibly boring official business.

A voice called out to me from behind, saving me from having to be involved with that mess.

"Excuse me, Commander Airis?"

I turned around to find an elven woman standing there, Tatsuko Hirota, one of the scouting party members that stopped Julius and I in the woods. We had interacted a number of times on our trek south. She was assigned to Hanna's party, so a few of those times were in mock battles.

She was level headed, and had a never ending list of stories and experiences to share. I never asked, but Mei had told me that Tatsuko was older than she was—but because she was a full blooded elf, that she was still very young in relative terms.

"Oh hey, Tatsuko. Did you need something?"

"If you have a moment, I was hoping we could talk about the Terror Demon."

I shuddered at the thought of such a monstrous thing. Terror Demons were an unexpected conversation starter.

"Oh? What did you want to talk about?"

"Mei and I had been combining notes about them. She and I both remember when Tolin was still a functioning city... Did you know I even lived here for some time?"

"I didn't know that. I'll have to pick your brain about the city one of these nights."

"My family fled to the Empire after our village was destroyed during the Apocalypse... The forests of The Vale were one of the first places destroyed by the monster attacks."

"The Empire took in our clans on the condition that our militias would enlist in their armies, and so I found myself serving as a Battle-Mage in the Sixth Legion, stationed at Tolin. We received news of devastating losses along the western front. The whole war was one tactical withdrawal after another, until the City of Light itself fell. A runner arrived one morning with news that Vanixia had been evacuated after Emperor Alexandros had been killed, and that his son, Theodin, was en route to Tolin with the survivors."

I sighed heavily at the mention of my father's name. It was odd to hear a story about him that was before the founding of Axio, and it jarred me slightly. Tatsuko paused her story, allowing me a moment to clear my head.

"That night, they passed through the city. We had fortified as best we could, but the garrison commander ordered the bulk of the city to follow on north after the rest of the survivors. My legion and two others left the city to escort the civilians. We caught up with Theodin's group crossing the mountain pass. Some of the officers there had seen the Terror Demons first-hand in combat."

Hailey and Hanna walked over to listen in on our conversation. Tatsuko continued on.

"So, you could say I have some experience regarding them. These things are on another level than us. They were usually the commanding force behind a monster invasion. If we do come up against one it's going to take everything we've got to stand a chance. They are incredibly fast—so fast that even elven rangers couldn't keep track of them."

I took a moment to absorb the story. If the Terror Demons did act like a commander to a horde of monsters, then there may not be multiple to deal with. Rather, just a single one.

"I'm not expecting them to be easy, but our Divisionals have thirty years of experience dealing with monsters and beasts."

"Commander, I'm not saying the people here aren't experienced. I just want to make sure that everyone is fully prepared to face this threat. If one of those demons is still here, we're about to walk into a literal hellscape."

Hanna jumped in, "Don't worry, Tatsuko, I'll brief all the teams tonight about what we're facing. Our scouting parties should return soon and we'll have a better idea of what to expect."

Tatsuko saluted and left the command tent.

Hailey's stomach growled, prompting Hanna to let out a loud laugh. Hailey ribbed her with an elbow.

"Shut up, Hanna, I'm starving! Can we go find some food now?"

We found the rest of our party at the mess hall. I grabbed one of the hot meals that was being served, some sort of meat and bread, and found a seat next to Julius.

"So, you were busy today?"

"..."

Julius didn't respond. He was staring at his plate, softly prodding his meal with a fork.

"Whatcha doing there, Julius?"

"Trying to figure out what kind of meat this is."

Mei lifted her head up from her plate, "It's field marmot."

Julius' face twisted with a trace of disgust.

"Oh."

SEVEN

TOLIN WAS LAID OUT IN FOUR MAJOR DISTRICTS. Market, Port, Garrison, and Residential. The city was surrounded by tall, castellated walls; and each district was separated by smaller walls with a single gatehouse acting as the point of entry from one district to another. A number of towers lined the walls that overlooked the city.

The market district began directly past the front gates. Two main roads winded through the city from there; the residential district was to the west, and the port district was to the east.

Beyond the rows of homes and villas in the residential district was another gate, that led to the garrison district which housed the Citadel. The size of that stronghold would allow tens of thousands of soldiers to be stationed there with ease.

In the east laid the sprawling port district, with its quay walls jutting out against the ocean waves. Warehouses and artisan crafting workshops dotted this district, it was the industry backbone of the lost Empire's expanding frontier.

South of the port district, a massive steel-reinforced stone bridge spanned the length of the channel mouth. This engineering marvel linked to Tolin's sister city, Ingmont, on the other side of the gulf.

It was late when the scouting parties reported back in.

The teams that scouted the walls around the city reported no hostile creatures and very little activity as a whole.

One party provided a detailed sketch of a section of the city wall that had crumbled near where a river ran through the city. The river flowed along the residential and market district border wall. They indicated that the damage appeared to be more likely from erosion, than from any monster.

The four parties that searched the city were much busier avoiding hostiles to fully accomplish their reconnaissance mission. After taking in all the reports, our adversaries included packs of wild dogs, demon hounds, and Capradaemns.

I asked each scouting party the same question, and each party had the same response...

Nobody saw anything that they would describe as a Terror Demon.

Once the last scouting group left and we were alone Hailey let out a sigh, whether it was in relief or from stress I wasn't sure.

"Airis, do you think we're in the clear?"

"In the clear from what?"

"I mean, do you think we'll have to deal with that... Terror Demon?"

"It could just be hiding. Or it may have moved on. We don't have any actionable intel that can confirm either of those two options."

She sat down and buried her face into the table. Her mumbled words could barely be made out.

"Being in command sucks."

I laughed and gently brushed my hand through my hair.

"It really does sometimes."

"If I had known it would be this stressful I... I wouldn't have taken this position!"

Hailey raised her head up and looked at me in alarm as she blurted that out.

She started to push her chair back but I grabbed a hold of her shoulders. I raised an eyebrow at her, and in response she tried to pull away from me.

"Not fair. Let me go!"

She squirmed with all her might, but couldn't get out of my grasp.

"Not until you explain what you meant."

Hailey crossed her arms, "Hmph."

"You can sit here and pout, but I'm not letting you go till I find out what you're hiding from me."

"Fine, but the next secret you try to keep I'm gonna pester you until you tell me. I heard about an opening in Third Division when Commander Morgan was thinking of retiring. It came with orders to Axio, and I applied to be closer to you!"

Ohhhhh... wait what!?—

Before I had the time to really digest what she had said, the canvas door flung open wildly and Julius ran into the command tent. He bore a grim expression, and even grimer news.

"Hostiles engaged the guards at the gate. A lot of them."

"Shit. Where are the others?"

"They're already there, and now that I've found you two we have to get out there!"

Hailey and I hurried after him, rushing out of the camp. The evening sun was setting, there would only be an hour of good light remaining.

The sounds of battle echoed over the hills.

Two wounded soldiers limped past us as we rode to the barricade. A fiery explosion flared in front of us followed by a tower of smoke that rose up into the sky.

The air around us thickened as we descended into the Aethermist that covered the battlefield.

The Divisional guards had hastily repositioned the barricades to form three hardened defensive positions.

From these makeshift positions, archers were taking opportunities to pick off their aggressors. On the front, a shieldwall had formed and was preparing to charge forward.

Humanoid figures swarmed from the battered gates. Their heads, however, were anything but human—more goat-like. Long, twisted horns arched back from their foreheads. Sickly pale skin was pulled taut against muscular upper frames with thick hair covering their lower halves, ending at cloven feet.

A quick scan of the demons revealed they weren't as formidable as they seemed. But with sheer multitude of them, this was still going to be a hard pressed battle.

TARGET	STATISTICS	VALUES
CAPRADAEMN	HEALTH	175 / 175
	STAMINA	92 / 100
	MAGICKA	50 / 50

Just as Julius had said, our party members were already here. Mei was taking shots with the other archers. Soren and Alistaire were among the shieldwall, swords at the ready. The only person I didn't have eyes on was Luke—and as soon as that thought came to mind, Luke's voice crackled to life from the Communirune in my ear.

"Glad to see you made it, Commander. The gate was overrun by a surprise attack, but we have managed to keep the defensive line."

I looked out among the pockets of red-clothed Divisionals, but still couldn't find where he was hiding.

"Hey Luke, good to hear your voice. Where are you?"

"Eastern barricade. I'm spotting for the rangers here. None of these bastards are getting past us."

An unsettling chill ran down my spine. The pressure of the Aethermist was increasing, the demons were about to make another charge.

But, before I had a chance to warn him, Julius had already run forward and was shouting orders.

"Alcotts, Jameson. Get your asses over here. Let's go! Form up on me. Alcotts you're in cycle first. Jameson you stay two lengths back and watch our hides."

The two boys fell in with Julius. With all those training drills every night and morning, they had become very proficient in following Julius' orders. As they moved forward, It felt like they had been fighting together for years.

Their strides were perfectly in-step with each other. Both of the junior warriors had picked up cycling quickly in training.

Ear piercing screams emanated from the gate and a horde of capradaemns spilled out into the battlefield.

A warcry roared from the shieldwall, and they began pushing forward steadily. A flare spell rose in the air behind me, prompting a hail of arrows that peppered down upon the demons.

Divisional arrowheads were designed to inflict the most damage possible to monsters and demons; triple-bladed broadheads with another set of blades that winged out behind it. They caused a tremendous amount of damage, basically guaranteeing that a target would start to bleed out. In most cases they would leave a limb crippled if struck.

The advancing shieldwall made contact, blade and spear met claw and fang.

Hailey called out to me while she was casting a spell.

"Get up there and backup our boys. I can manage healing for now. I'll call out to you if I need your help."

I nodded at her and stepped to move away, but quickly stopped.

I traced a focusing sigil and channeled energy to my palms. I placed one on her right shoulder.

"Peer past the infinite veil. Let the power hidden within our being come forth, Brilliance!"

Violet light enveloped us both and she grinned widely.

Julius, Soren, and Alistaire were to the west of the shieldwall. I took a position on the eastern side, giving Luke a clear line of sight to me. This way, I could call out for support if I got into anything too troubling.

The shieldwall formation was a standard pushing defensive formation. This one was on the smaller side, only being three rows by fifteen columns with three officers in the rear. They advanced in a wedge, gaining a few inches of ground against each demon they felled.

Arrows continued to inflict casualties, and the demons began to act more erratically. Instead of engaging directly with the force ahead of them, they started to focus their aggression on the archers raining hell down on them.

A group of five demons charged at the opening between myself and the shieldwall. A red glow illuminated each of them and a cry rang out far above me.

I unsheathed my blade, the dark-crimson flames erupted in a dazzling display of ferocity.

Valiance, Mei's ebon feathered companion had used her MARK TARGET ability. In addition to making them much easier to detect, it highlighted weak spots with an intense light.

I readied my blade in front of me, in an attack stance, leaning forward and crouching at the waist. I balanced myself for a quick slash and waited to strike. Once the first demon was close enough, I burst into motion.

My blade cut upwards in a diagonal arcing slash through the monster. Flames trailed behind the swing, erupting aggressively once the blade finished rending the flesh. The dark fire spread out in a nova, engulfing the group of demons.

They screamed in pain as their flesh burned in magickal fire.

The target of my BLADE SLASH was completely eviscerated by the attack. I had aimed at the brightest spot on its body, which happened to be its lower abdomen. The bloody carnage was made more appalling by the foul smell of burning flesh.

Nobody had seen the effect of SOULFIRE yet. Julius and I had only been training with practice weapons. We expected that it would be intense—but I was surprised at the power of the ability. The reactionary effect of the nearby Divisionals indicated that it was more than awe inspiring. A throng of slack-jawed soldiers gave their impressions.

"By the Celestials!"

"A single strike took all five of those bastards!"

An officer called out a rallying cry, "Witness the power of our Commander! These demonspawn stand no chance, we'll cut them all down!"

The soldiers in the shieldwall let out a boisterous cry and advanced further.

I quickly reviewed my combat log for a detailed breakdown.

» BLADE SLASH HITS, INFLICTING MODERATE (132) DAMAGE

» BLADE SLASH CAUSES MAJOR WOUNDS

» SOULFIRE HITS, INFLICTING MAJOR (132) DAMAGE

» SOULFIRE SPLASHES, INFLICTING MAJOR (132) DAMAGE

» SOULFIRE CAUSES MAJOR WOUNDS

By the Celestials, that effect is staggering.

The splashing damage from the SOULFIRE looked like it applied the full amount of damage to nearby enemies, rather than a reduced area of effect like most Combat Class spells. I wasn't sure if the effect did major damage because of the major wounds, or if that's just standard for this ability.

Fortunately for me, there was a horde of these goatman-demons for me to test this out on.

My blade slashed through them, always followed by its ravenous flames that engulfed each target. Without fail, each swing resulted in fire bursting outwards to consume anything close by.

After the first few groups I stopped checking the combat logs. Every time SOULFIRE hit, it caused major damage and applied the same level of wounds.

» BLADE SLASH HITS, INFLICTING MODERATE (156) DAMAGE
» BLADE SLASH CAUSES MAJOR WOUNDS
» SOULFIRE HITS, INFLICTING MAJOR (156) DAMAGE
» SOULFIRE SPLASHES, INFLICTING MAJOR (156) DAMAGE
» SOULFIRE CAUSES MAJOR WOUNDS
» BLADE SLASH HITS, INFLICTING MODERATE (98) DAMAGE
» BLADE SLASH CAUSES MAJOR WOUNDS
» SOULFIRE HITS, INFLICTING MAJOR (98) DAMAGE
» SOULFIRE SPLASHES, INFLICTING MAJOR (98) DAMAGE
» SOULFIRE CAUSES MAJOR WOUNDS

Within an hour, we had control over the gatehouse. The sun was now barely visible on the horizon. Countless demon corpses lied slain in the dirt—not a single Divisional soldier had died. Though some were moderately injured, but not severely enough to warrant expending more magicka from the healers.

The injured were loaded onto carriages and carts and sent back to the main camp to be overseen by the field hospital staff.

The remaining Divisionals were completely exhausted. The majority of guardsmen leaned on their shields and spears, breathing heavily.

Even past their limits, a few of the guards were fawning over Soren and Alistaire, who had enraptured the group with their flashy combat cycle switching.

Those two never had formal weapons training, instead, they'd developed a style very similar to Julius'. It looked like they were competing at a tournament with every strike. Every attack had an elegant motion to it.

It was truly something to watch the three of them in training, and I'm sure it was at another level in real combat.

The guardsmen dispersed when I walked over, saving me the trouble of trying to figure out how to get my party members back.

"You boys look like you're in one piece."

Alistaire grinned, "Not a scratch on us."

Soren nodded.

"Looks like you've gained some admirers as well." I pointed at the guardsmen who were walking away.

"Hah! Yeah we did. Soren and me hit those demons like thunder strikes! Pow! Pow! Pow!"

Alistaire punched his fists in the air.

"Lightning strikes..." Soren interjected quietly.

"Yeah lightning strikes, Soren! You knew what I meant, whatever, that battle was intense!"

"Uh huh, well Lightning Striker, how about you take some of this energy and focus it on making sure this gatehouse is secure?"

Alistaire kicked at the ground with his boot in a 'Awh, do I have to?' response.

Soldiers were scrambling around us, busy repositioning barricades to form a new defensive position.

I laughed, "Look, just make sure the guards moving the barricades don't have anything nasty sneak up on them."

The two of them scurried off to help a pair of soldiers struggling with a heavy steel-reinforced spike barricade.

The main gatehouse to Tolin stood at a menacing forty-five feet tall. It was designed to elicit a sense of admiration and awe towards the former empire that built the city. Though in part it was built to be defensive, its main features were more dramatic than practical. The vaulted stone ceiling was crumbling, revealing the rotting lumber of the floor above.

Hailey, Luke, and Mei joined us at the gatehouse. They all looked healthy, though Hailey looked a little drained.

The archetype for priest healing was expensive, long cast time, spells that applied an area of effect heal in a wide range. Where I, as a paladin, could get away with using less than ten magicka for each of my minor healing spells, Hailey would spend thirty or more per each basic healing spell. The trade off for efficient healing being an area effect was well worth it to most Divisional healers however.

I swiped at my wrist to activate my OVERSIGHT ability to see how she was fairing.

PARTY MEMBERS	STATISTICS	VALUES
HAILEY BROOKS	HEALTH	60 / 60
	STAMINA	115 / 185
	MAGICKA	225 / 540

She definitely had her work cut out for her. With a little over three-hundred magicka spent she would have cast ten or so spells in an hour. That kind of mental drain was hard for any caster if you didn't have an absurdly high SANITY attribute.

Even battle hardened war-mages couldn't pelt an opposing force with a barrage of spells.

The best magickians in Axio could only conjure two or three action class offensive spells every ten minutes without succumbing to magicka feedback.

Feedback made even the worst case of brain freeze feel like a calming massage in comparison.

Her head was probably throbbing in pain.

"Hails, you doing okay?"

"..."

Her response was walking straight into me, pressing her head against my breastplate and letting out the tiniest whimper that only I could hear.

"Nnhh-uh."

Well that answers that.

A hand clapped my shoulder and Luke's voice came from behind me.

"That was an incredible display there, Commander," He whistled softly, "Those demons didn't know what hit them."

"I was just as surprised as anyone else. I'm still not entirely sure how the sword's ability effect works, but I think I've got the general idea down."

The damage the blade inflicted was doubled by the SOULFIRE effect, that damage was then splashed to any nearby enemies. What I didn't know was if the effect applied a major wound to any foe, or if these demons were just susceptible to that particular effect.

I was getting lost in thought, when Valiance let out a high-pitched screech above the gatehouse. We all looked at Mei expectantly. I wasn't sure if they could communicate somehow through their soulmate bond, but you never know what sort of weird tricks an Elf could pull.

"Danger is approaching." she said blankly.

I felt and heard Hailey groan, but it was quiet, muffled by my armor. The rest of the party was still unaware of her condition.

"Any chance you can elaborate on the type of 'danger'?" Luke asked.

"Monsters." she shrugged.

Luke sighed, and gave Mei a pat on the shoulder, "Really narrowed it down there."

Julius picked up his shield, "The soldiers aren't ready for another fight like that last one. They'll buckle against the next wave. We should take a position in the courtyard past the gatehouse and keep whatever is coming busy while they rest."

Soren and Alistaire both shrugged and followed Julius, who was already walking away. Mei followed closely behind them.

"He's something else, ya' know that?" Luke said flatly, staring at Julius.

"What do you mean?"

"He organized the guards during the first attack—and ordered moving the barricades and shieldwall in absolutely no time. Before the first demon even took a step past the gates, we were ready for them. No doubt that the only reason anyone here is alive, is because he was around."

"That's Julius for you. He's not just a pretty face. There is a reason he's my vice-commander."

Luke continued to stare as the rest of our party walked through the ruined gateway.

"Next fight should be easy, Hails. You only have to watch the six of us. I'll assist if you need me to."

Another pitiful groan echoed up from my breastplate. Hailey stomped her feet as she followed me and Luke through the gate to face the new threat.

No rest for the weary, they say.

The gateway opened up into the market square. The city's main street continued south. The ruined exterior of shops stood along the promenade. Overgrown foliage entangled every surface. Roots broke their way through the paved streets, making the whole place a hazard.

The sun was setting fast, the light was barely bright enough to illuminate the courtyard ahead.

"Source of light that dwells among the veiled. Come forth and guide our way, Radiance!"

Bright golden light washed over us as AURA OF LIGHT took effect. In addition to its increased healing spell efficiency, the aura provided a small radius of visible light around each of us, allowing us to see for about fifteen feet in any direction clearly—though the light faded quickly past that point.

The open market square had little in the form of cover or defensive positioning. We were in the open. But before I had a chance to bring up my discomfort in our current state of affairs, a new situation developed.

Guttural howls pierced my ears, and the faint red glow of demonic eyes appeared around us. More of the goatmen charged out of the surrounding buildings, this time accompanied by demon-hounds—Identical to the two that Julius and I had fought a week ago.

"Hey Julius, good thing you remembered your shield this time." I teased.

The snarky response that I was expecting didn't come. Instead, a soft silver light emanated from his shield. The light grew in intensity until his entire shield was glowing. The shield itself started to shift. It warped in shape, now extending down past his knees to a sharp curved-point and up above his shoulders. The top of the shield jutted forward in what looked like the face of a bird of prey. The face of the shield was a flashy crimson-red, and was emblazoned with a silver feathery pattern. Three ruby-jeweled sockets adorned the crimson-red face of the shield.

"Light, grant me Strength. For in Strength I find Power. In Power I create Unity. In Unity, I serve the righteous and bring forth justice to these tainted lands. Despair forces of darkness, Silver Bulwark!"

The silver glow that had been building up as Julius spoke his incantation, burst—flowing out around us and forming a bubble.

» YOU ARE AFFECTED BY A PROTECTIVE BARRIER.

"What in the Aether is that!?"

Julius flashed me with the largest and by far, the most annoying grin to date.

"You weren't the only one to get a new toy from that Dwarven lady."

"Are you kidding me!? This whole time you've been keeping some crazy superb skill from me!" I huffed.

I cannot believe this man!

He turned to address the rest of our party and started calling out orders.

"Stay inside the field, and any damaging effects will be reduced. Soren, you're up first with me. Mei, pick off these hounds. There are too many of them, their charge ability can do some serious damage."

Soren jumped into action with Julius and they began to engage the oncoming legion. Soren's flashy swings perfectly mirrored Julius', It was like watching the performance of skilled artisans. Each strike was deliberate and perfectly timed.

Mei's arrow shots produced a deep 'thwang' from her longbow, echoed by the 'thud' of a devastating impact. Each arrow loosed resulted in a near perfect headshot. Her arrows were a complex variation that were issued to an elite core of rangers, called Waystriders. They were, in terms of lethality, twice as effective as their standard Divisional counterparts.

Luke had disappeared from sight and was prowling out in the darkness looking for unaware targets to ambush.

Alistaire was on our left flank waiting for his turn to switch in.

I took the right flank. I held my sword with the blade low, ready to counter an attack and follow through with a forward strike.

A demon hound lept at me from the darkness, and I swung my sword upwards. The blade connected with the hound mid lunge and cut deep. It impacted against bone and knocked the hound off course.

Flames engulfed the demon and illuminated the surrounding area. The newly lit corner of the market square turned into an archery range as Mei let loose a volley of arrows at a cluster of newly exposed demons, now illuminated by MARK TARGET.

I used the opening to engage my own new targets, a group of goatmen who were skulking behind a ruined market stall.

I charged forward, lunging at the closest demon.

My blade sank deep into its chest and flames erupted from the cavity within, taking its allies down with it.

We pushed deeper into the market square slaughtering the demon hordes with gross efficiency.

Mei's voice came over the Communirune.

"Commander, I'm sensing a change in the weather coming in fast. Winds are picking up speed—we may be in the middle of a storm in minutes."

I slashed through another demon, flames gorged on another victim. A bright flash of light crawled across the sky revealing the true level of annihilation—hundreds of demons laid slain. But the lightning also revealed something more worrying.

A massive shape was moving through the city streets. Its towering body could be seen lording over the roofs of the dilapidated square.

A rush of wind almost pushed me over. The drumming of raindrops impacting the ground grew in intensity until the rainstorm was on top of us, soaking the square completely.

Each time the lightning flashed, the shape of the approaching foe grew larger.

Luke emerged from the shadows, "Commander, we need to go. This storm is getting worse by the second, and I don't want one of these roofs coming up and burying us in debris."

"I don't think we have that option." I said as thundering footsteps shook the ground beneath us.

An ear piercing screech paralyzed me, and incredible pain flared against my forehead. Luke's face was stuck in a twist of pain as well. His hands were holding his head and a weak cry escaped his lips.

Hailey cried out and dropped to the ground, clutching her head. Soren and Alistaire faltered momentarily, but composed themselves quickly. Julius didn't even appear to be fazed by the noise.

The monstrous figure stepped closer, its true shape now in view. An Ettin. It stood over twenty-feet tall. Broad, musclebound shoulders supported two grotesque bald humanoid heads. Both heads looked almost identical, save for the unique scarring that bespeckled their faces. Eyes as black as the Void peered at us through the fog.

Its arms stretched downwards, gripping an enormous crude mace that looked like it was created by hammering large iron spikes through the mast of a ship. The Ettin was without any heavy protective equipment, wearing only a weathered loincloth.

A large chain was wrapped around its waist, along which were strands of rope. Each rope ended with a knotted skull that dangled in place as the monster advanced.

TARGET	STATISTICS	VALUES
GIGAS	HEALTH	4350 / 4350
	STAMINA	1000 / 1000
	MAGICKA	0 / 0

With a wild swing of its giant mace, it struck a small building, shattering the tiled roof and splintering the wooden frame. Gigas roared a guttural battle-cry and shadows moved in the darkness around us.

Julius readied his sword. He took a wide stance with his arm pulled back, the blade angled up sharply. Soren and Alistaire lunged forward swinging their swords in a diagonal strike aimed at Gigas' legs. Its mace swung between them, colliding with the blades. Both of them were knocked back by the strength of the blow.

Out of the corner of my eye I watched their health drop substantially.

Julius jumped in without hesitation. Gigas was still recovering from its own swing, and didn't have a chance to block the attack.

His sword connected with the demon's torso. A clean hit. The deep cut glowed with golden light from Julius' weapon imbuement.

"Groaaaaah!"

Gigas bellowed with fury and staggered backwards. Light glinted from both sides of its legs. Soren and Alistaire had recovered and were taking advantage of the momentarily distracted demon's lack of attention.

I took off in a run to catch up with the fighters.

As I passed by Hailey, her staff flared brightly with golden energy as she began casting a spell.

"Blessed and divine light, lend me your strength. Through me, channel the goodwill of your power and deliver them from harm. Healing Grace!"

A runic sigil formed in the space above her and rays of light beamed down on Soren and Alistaire.

Luke shimmered in the light and he faded out of sight as he activated a stealth ability. Moments later he reappeared near the darkness beyond the aura's reach, eviscerating a group of smaller demons that had encroached on our battle.

He vanished once again into the dark and more bleating screams were heard.

Turning my attention back to the bigger threat, the giant had recovered and its club came crashing down overhead the three swordsmen. Julius managed to jump back, pushing off of an overturned stone slab. Soren grabbed Alistaire by the wrist and pulled him narrowly out of the attack's radius.

I was now close enough to hear Julius hiss expletives at the monster.

If we put pressure on the giant with all of us at close range, it's going to continue using these power attacks.

We watched as the monster heaved its mighty weapon from the crater the blow had formed. Maybe keeping pressure on the giant was not the greatest plan. With a simple thought I opened a mental channel to the party over the Communirunes.

"Spread out and attack during the recovery period after each attack. Julius, see if you can taunt the thing to give us an opening to strike."

I heard him mumble something, but he wasn't close enough for me to make it out. But it had sounded like he may not be enjoying this fight. I was positive that stupid grin of his was long gone.

"Come on you ugly bastard, over here! Rooaaah!"

The Ettin turned its attention down towards Julius. It lifted up its weapon and prepared to swing.

I lunged forward to get a quick strike in while it was distracted. The flames of my blade licked at its flesh as the ebony metal cut through its thick skin. As my sword came free and I readied for another attack, I was stopped as my plan fell apart...

The giant had stopped its swing short and was now turning around, its weapon racing at me with an incredible momentum.

Julius dived in front of me. Now stuck between the impending mace attack. He had tossed his sword and was gripping his shield with both gauntleted hands.

"Light, grant me Strength. For in Strength I find—"

Julius' incantation was cut off as the giant's mace impacted his shield. The force knocked him off his feet sending him tumbling backwards.

The attack was deflected slightly, but not nearly enough as the weapon bearing down on me struck me hard in the right shoulder.

"Shaaaaaa!"

An unearthly screech clawed its way from my throat as the metal plate was sheared from my breastplate. The jagged metal was driven downwards across my arm, slicing a deep gash through my bicep.

My stamina drained away into the blackzone and I was left writhing on the ground, paralyzed with a stun effect.

My left hand released its grip on my blade as I grabbed onto my shoulder. The sword clattered to the ground, dark crimson flames flaring brightly. An icon blinked into existence next to my interface and a message displayed in my combat log.

» YOU HAVE BEEN STUNNED.
» YOU ARE AFFLICTED WITH EXHAUSTION RANK I.
» YOU ARE SUFFERING FROM A CRIPPLED ARM.

Shit. Can't heal this wound until I get my arm set.

I craned my neck using every bit of strength that I had remaining, trying to look up.

A shimmering figure in the distance was barely visible. Luke was still dealing with the horde of demons that flooded in around us. Soren was on the giant's flank. He was charging in for an attack, sword high above his head—

"Watch out!"

Luke's voice echoed through the courtyard and rang out in my ear as the Communirune crackled with feedback at the surprise shout.

I turned my head back to where I last saw him. Three demon hounds had skirted past him and were barreling down the cobbled roadway straight at me.

Double shit.

The stun effect was wearing off and I tried to stand. My footing didn't hold and I staggered forward, catching myself from hitting the ground face first by extending my left arm.

"Aaaah!"

I cried out in pain as my right arm twisted from the impact. I rolled left and swung backwards to sit on the ground.

I lifted my left arm and channeled a moderate amount of magick through it.

"Righteous Fire!"

A bolt of golden flame struck the closest hound, exploding and taking it out of the fight.

The remaining two snarled, unphased, continued to close in.

Golden light coalesced around my fist, I readied another HOLY BOLT.

"Righteous Fire!"

Another hound was taken down in an explosive light show. I reached out for my sword, grabbing it just as the final hound lunged at me. I brought my blade up to attempt a deflecting parry and caught the beast's jowls with it.

Vicious claws ripped and tore at me as the demon snarled violently. I pushed back with my limited strength in an effort to free myself. My stamina bar flashed wildly in my periphery.

The beast's legs found purchase in the pavers beneath us and I was pushed down onto my back, knocking the breath out of me. I wheezed hard, and the hound freed itself from the entanglement with my blade.

My health bar was now flashing almost as wildly as the stamina bar below it.

PARTY MEMBERS	STATISTICS	VALUES
AIRIS VANIXI (OPERATOR)	HEALTH	17 / 90
	STAMINA	0 / 245
	MAGICKA	275 / 350

I was now in a position where I was praying my armor would absorb the damage long enough that someone could arrive to help. I raised my good arm up to protect my face from the impending attack.

"Get the *fuck* off of my Commander!"

The brutish yell made me drop my arm to see who had shouted it.

A plated sabaton connected with the hound's midsection knocking it away from me. I followed the leg back to its owner, and looked upon the face of the ever quiet and reserved Soren.

He was panting hard, and beads of sweat cascaded down his face. His normally soft and passive features were gone, replaced with a bloodcrazed fury.

Soren brandished his sword and thrust it forward, sinking into the demon's nape. He yanked the blade upwards and cut through the spine and connective tissues, the demon's head rolled free.

I couldn't do anything but stare in bewilderment at the scene in front of me. Soren wiped the blood from his sword on his uniform's coattail. He sheathed his weapon and turned to me.

The blood rage had faded away, and his soft smile had taken residence once more.

He held his arm out for me, "Allow me to assist you. I'll help you over to Commander Brooks."

We hobbled over towards Hailey. She was already running to us at a sprint. The look of panic radiated off her face as a palpable aura. She clutched me tightly and traded Soren as my primary supporter.

"Easy now, I've got you."

Her gentle words soothed my pain. Her own kind of unique magick.

"Sit down, let's get you patched up." she ordered, helping me down. She looked at Soren, who nodded and took my limp arm.

He counted down calmly, "Three... Two... One—"

POP!

The golden glow of Hailey's magick was already building up around her hands. She placed them gingerly on me, "Divine light, Deliver her from harm. Healing Grace!"

The best way to describe the feeling of a wound being healed by magick was told to me by a senior instructor at VxA: A dance of a thousand needles around the wound.

Normally, a wound on its own heals by the tissue slowly stitching itself back together. But through magick the tissue is forced to stretch and replicate under extreme stress, rapidly accelerated, in seconds.

I gritted my teeth as the pain of my wounded arm abated, though just replaced by the pain the magick was wracking my arm with.

It was perilous to keep fighting without a plan. If we didn't come up with something it was likely one of us would die here. And at this point that someone might be me.

Hailey's hand lingered on my now healed arm. Her face looked pale, but her expression had relaxed. She didn't look nearly as unnerved. I reached up and clasped my own around hers.

"Nice job, Hails. I'm good as new thanks to you."

She shuddered, letting out a pained sigh.

"I... nevermind—"

She got up from her stooped position and held out her hand. With her help I was back on my feet.

My uniform coat had been torn and ripped to shreds. The coattails were hanging loosely around my waist. I pulled my dagger from its sheath and quickly cut the damaged fabric free.

A cold gust of wind blew through the courtyard, making me instantly regret that decision—but a little cold air ruffling my skirt was a better situation than tripping over the ruined strips of coat.

My full attention was now back on the priority threat, that was the twenty-foot tall siege weapon of a demon. The boys had been chipping away at its health consistently, and one solid push might be enough to take it down.

I spotted Mei across the courtyard. She had fallen back, giving distance between herself, the ettin.

She was holding her bowstring back in a draw, arrow knocked. A greenish glow was building around the tip.

Her voice carried in the wind, the words felt like they were being echoed by the gale around us. The sharp inflections and cadence of elvish

"*EGI ADVICAE QUTI DUX. STELLAE IMPERIAE. EXCIPI CALX!*"

The intensity of the wind grew around her, rushing in and blowing her hair and cloak wildly. A soft metallic sound rang out and the arrow tip changed from a dull steel color to a brilliant white. She must have a direct mental link to me, because she was already preparing for a final push.

Her voice came over my communirune, "Airis, get ready to strike."

I rushed the demon again. Adrenaline coursed through me, though my nerves were alight with fear.

Mei spoke a single word. Her voice was so soft and calm that I almost faltered.

"Now."

As she was expecting her command to be executed precisely when given. I lunged with my sword pulled back, and swung it forward with all the strength I could muster.

Mei loosed her arrow and with a loud crack that shattered the air. It flew forwards so fast that it practically materialized in the demon's chest. The arrow struck at the center of a bright red illuminated glow.

The impact caved the beast's chest in, flesh and bone blew out over the street below. An instant later, my blade struck the impact site. My sword carved hungrily through the exposed tissue. Flames engulfed the cavity—but these flames were different—glittering particles of crimson-red raced out across the demon's skin.

Gigas cried out in another ear piercing screech. This time however, we weren't struck with a paralysis effect.

This time the demon was crying out in pain. The critical strike effect of SOULFIRE was burning every nerve the monster had.

A quick succession of blade slashes flashed, as my trio of swordsmen struck the demon with a series of combination strikes. Soren and Alistaire attacked with an impressive display of speed and agility.

Julius' strike was a heavy slash that made a shuddering crunching noise as it hit. The giant demon stood frozen in place for a moment before it crashed down to the ground.

The earth shook as the mountainous beast fell.

A deafening thunderclap reverberated against the city's stone walls. Like a supernatural call of retreat, the horde of demons fell back and we were left standing alone in the market square arena.

The heavy weight of my rain soaked armor overcame my resolve. Fatigue flooded in and I collapsed to the ground. I groaned loudly as my head throbbed.

"Uhhhhhggggh!"

I was joined by my party members, they walked over and sat down in the rain with me to catch their breath. The rain fell harder and the wind grew fiercer, but we didn't move a muscle. We leaned against each other, stacked together in a pile of exhaustion.

Soren broke the silence, his boyish voice wavering and broken, not a hint of the crazed berserker that saved me earlier.

"I—I can't believe we survived that..."

A wild fit of laughter came from Alistaire. His hearty laugh was contagious and soon we were all lightly chuckling.

Julius was the first to stand, he stretched his arm out to help me up, "Let's get the hell out of here. The forward guard should be able to handle it from here. Doubtful anything will show its face tonight after this."

I eyed the fallen ettin.

I was confident that the beast didn't have pockets, so I doubted it carried any notable loot—but I did make a mental note to tell the quartermaster back in camp to send someone out to gather anything of use from its corpse.

We left the courtyard, and passed a squad of guardsmen standing at the gateway. Their faces bore wide smiles and wicked grins. They must have watched us fell the massive ettin.

On the other side of the gates we were greeted with the sounds of loud cheering that drowned out the drone of the wind and rain.

"They slayed a giant!"

"Hail our mighty Commander! Airis, The Crimson Blade."

"The Crimson Blade!"

"With the Commander on our side, nothing can stop us!"

My body ached in pain, but I kept my shoulders high as we walked through the crowd of fatigued faces. Their calls for 'The Crimson Blade' gave me a short burst of adrenaline.

Once we passed the mass of recovering soldiers Hailey slumped against me, making each step an awkward stumble. We climbed up onto a horse and my muscles turned to jelly. I melted into a puddle of slime in my saddle and she jostled around behind me. Beyond exhausted, the singular goal in my mind was to get back to camp and fall into my bed.

Hanna was there to meet us as we entered the camp. Alistaire and Luke began to recount our heroics while the rest of us walked past them like living corpses.

Hanna tried to stop Hailey and me to talk about something—Hailey just grabbed my hand and pulled me forward. She mumbled at Hanna that we could talk in the morning, and that she wanted someone to come by and take our gear to the blacksmith.

When we approached our tent, Rias rushed over to meet us. Her bloodshot eyes said enough and I closed my mouth before saying anything stupid.

"You jerk!" She pounded a fist against my chestplate, "You left without saying anything and I was worried. When the injured soldiers got back, I—"

Her voice cutoff as she gawked at my ruined uniform and damaged armor. She reached out towards my right shoulder, touching the ripped cloth sleeve where a metal plate should've been.

"W-What in the Aether happened to you!? Are you okay?"

"I'm okay. We had a little run in with something nasty. But your big sis handled it, no problem."

Rias pursed her lips and angled herself away from me, looking to Hailey expectantly.

Hailey weakly raised her hands up. "Hey don't get upset with me, I just healed everyone. Airis got herself all beat up on her own."

With a weak laugh I placed my arm around Rias and led her into the tent. "We're all fine. I think all three of us are probably exhausted, physically and emotionally, let's turn in for the night."

Rias huffed for a bit, but eventually settled down. She helped me struggle out of my equipment and fetched a cloth and wooden washbasin.

I barely managed to scrub off the grunge before collapsing into bed. The muscles in my arm spasmed momentarily causing me to twist awkwardly to my side.

Hailey stumbled back while taking off her boots, falling into bed on top of me. I groaned in discomfort, but didn't budge.

She curled up next to me and complained.

"I am so sore! My back hurts from carrying the party so hard."

She laughed loudly but doubled over to clutch her side.

"Ow—ow, it hurts to laugh."

I tried to think of a joke to lighten my own mood, but my brain was fried. After the stress of battle I was far from a humorous state. Instead, I buried my head in her shoulder, trying to hide my face—so that she couldn't see me break into tears. My voice trembled.

"I—I didn't think I'd make it... I was so afraid."

Hailey wrapped herself tightly around me.

"Me too."

I did eventually stop crying—but only because I had run out of tears. Not because I managed to somehow get control back over my emotions. I rolled over and acknowledged the soft blinking on my wrist, gently tapping it. A flood of new notifications filled my view.

» YOU HAVE GAINED IN POWER, YOUR ATTRIBUTES HAVE INCREASED:
» STRENGTH HAS INCREASED TO 32
　　» TOUGHNESS HAS INCREASED TO 26
　　» FORTITUDE HAS INCREASED TO 27
　　» COURAGE HAS INCREASED TO 45
» AGILITY HAS INCREASED TO 17
　　» SWIFTNESS HAS INCREASED TO 21
　　» PERCEPTION HAS INCREASED TO 10
　　» REFLEX HAS INCREASED TO 22
» AETHER HAS INCREASED TO 26
　　» INTELLIGENCE HAS INCREASED TO 36
　　» WISDOM HAS INCREASED TO 27
　　» SANITY HAS INCREASED TO 16
» VITALITY HAS INCREASED TO 32
　　» ENDURANCE HAS INCREASED TO 22
　　» STAMINA HAS INCREASED TO 34
　　» RESOLVE HAS INCREASED TO 42
» DEXTERITY HAS INCREASED TO 37
　　» CLEVERNESS HAS INCREASED TO 35
　　» FINESSE HAS INCREASED TO 33
　　» INGENUITY HAS INCREASED TO 45
» YOU HAVE GAINED IN POWER, YOU HAVE LEARNED A NEW SKILL:
» NEW ACTION CLASS COMBAT SKILL: WILD STRIKE

EIGHT

TAP. TAP. TAP.

A loud noise woke me up. My eyes were heavy with sleep and my head felt clouded. I pulled the sheets away from me and sat up in bed. Glancing over to my left, I found only empty space. Whipping my gaze to my right revealed another empty spot.

Hailey and Rias were missing.

It's fine. Maybe they're already up.

I took a deep breath and tried to calm down. My heart was racing. I rubbed the dryness away from my eyes. If everyone else was awake already then I'd need to hurry and get ready.

I swung my legs over and pushed myself out of bed. A creaking noise groaned from something wooden beneath my feet. Surprised at the sound I looked down to see what I had stepped on. Hardwood flooring covered the ground.

Wooden flooring where there should have been soft ground was only the start of discrepancies as I was wearing my leather boots, still scuffed and covered in blood from last night. My gaze followed up my legs, noting the torn leggings and torn over coat.

I clutched at my chest. My fingers traced down the deep grooves left behind from the snarling beasts teeth and claws.

The room I was in had a stark difference to the tent I had gone to sleep in. The walls were elegant with a regal flare, but they were showing age and wear as if this place had been abandoned long ago.

It was almost identical to one of the palace chambers in Axio.

Was I back in Axio?

No. That wasn't possible. This must be another one of those psychometric episodes again. But—I hadn't had any weird dreams after that first misplaced memory, so why now?

The sound that woke me up echoed through the chambers once more.

TAP. TAP. TAP.

Somebody was knocking on the door. I twisted around to find a massive metal door between two Doric pillars, overgrown in vines. I crept slowly through the room towards the doorway.

With every step forward, it seemed to move further away...

Was my vision blurred?

No. It was the door that was blurring, a dark mist cascaded down around it. Everything else in the room was in focus. The walls of the room fell away from the darkened ceiling and more black mist fell from above. I raised my arms up to shield my eyes. The mist settled along the floor, blurring everyone around me. The hardwood flooring faded away leaving a cracked stone pathway leading to the large door.

The black mist swayed around threateningly, mocking me.

BANG. BANG. BANG.

I pushed forward through the mist, magickal energy sparked off my skin as I moved. The mist thickened with each step, making it hard to breathe. I choked on it, and had to stop forcing my way. I narrowed my eyes to try to peer through it, though the doorway seemed to be just as far away as when I started. Further away even.

I tried to turn around, but some force pushed back hard against me, keeping me locked in place facing the receding door.

Dark-purple bolts of magick flared through the mist and struck the doorway. Runic sigils formed at the corners, lines formed linking them in an X. The runes pulsed quickly, flashing a rich and eerie violet.

The loud crack of thunder rang out. The pathway shook beneath me and started to collapse. Great chunks of rock split away and tumbled into the darkness. I tried to run away, but the same force pushed against me. I watched in horror as the empty void came ever closer.

The last stone I was standing on began to shake, my footing slipped and I fell to my knees. The stone began its own fall into the void, careening to the left. I grabbed at any break in the rock to keep myself from tumbling down into the dark—my fingers couldn't find purchase, and I fell into the void... Screaming.

I stopped falling, slamming onto a hard floor.

"Oooahh..." I groaned in pain, as my body slumped.

I was in the center of the palace chamber room. Heavy rain pattered against a window and the flash of lightning filled the room.

For a brief moment I caught a demonic visage staring at me from the corner. I stumbled backwards and fell against the bed. In the commotion, the lurking monster stirred. It leaned forwards out of the dark corner, into the lowly lit room.

The demon's head was a massive hammer-shaped wedge, ending in long, sharp pointed ears. Its eye flared with a rich purple glow that flickered like hungry flames.

A twisted sinister grin revealed jagged rows of dark fanged teeth. In its hunched stature, it was quite a few feet taller than an average human.

Then it stood.

Its legs bowed back, like some kind of enormous predatory bird. It came to stand at full height, towering over me at well over fifteen feet.

The looming figure pointed a clawed finger at me and traced out a series of runic-like symbols in the air.

Words hammered against my skull from a voice that seemed to come from inside my own head, "YOU WILL DIE."

Each letter inflicted a searing pain as if they were etched into my mind. Afflicted with incredible shock, from pain or pure terror, I was frozen in place, unable to move a single muscle.

Was this a warning, or a threat?

The demon stared at me, but did not move. If this was a threat it was clear that it was not able to carry it out right now or I would likely be dead already. My gaze drifted down to its hand, still pointed directly at me.

Bony-white claws the size of daggers were protruding from a four-fingered hand. It had a human-like thumb that with the three others, extended out a considerable length. Each appendage with claw was the size of a farming scythe.

I shuddered at the thought of being eviscerated by the terrible beast. It must have sensed my unease, because it traced out another set of runes.

This time though, no words assaulted my brain. Instead the space around us began to fade into a misty shadow.

Even the demon itself faded into the shadows, leaving me left alone in the chamber room with the two runic sigils.

My mind and heart were racing in overdrive.

What in the Aether was that thing? Where am I? This isn't just some nightmare or somebodies memory.

The sigils flickered and the shadows started to grow around me, engulfing all sources of light. At the rate they were spreading, the entire room would descend into darkness in seconds.

The sound of a clock echoed in my mind.

TICK. TOCK. TICK. TOCK.

TICK. TOCK. TICK. TOCK...

With each 'tick' the shadows danced faster until they engulfed everything. I was left floating in a black void, every direction I turned was the same empty nothingness.

A scraping noise stung my ears, and I saw a glow out of the corner of my eyes. I craned my neck to see more runic sigils coming to life.

"I WILL CONSUME YOU.", the words burned, even stronger than before, as they appeared in my mind.

"Arghhh! Celestials above!"

The unbearable pain left me doubled over, senses barely functioning. I forced my eyes open just in time to see a gaping maw of demonic fangs envelope me from the void below.

I cried out in terror—though my voice made no sound as I was swallowed whole...

"AAAAAAAAAAA—"

I shot upright, crying out in terror. The shirt I had went to bed in clung to my skin, it was drenched in sweat. My whole body trembled in fear. It took more than a moment to realize that Rias was clenched tightly around my right arm. Hailey looked up at me from the foot of the bed. Both of their faces were a mix of worry and panic.

Rias wrapped herself around me. I felt some of the panic reside and my nerves calmed. Now it was her body that was trembling.

"Y-you wouldn't wake up..." She whispered in my ear. "We weren't sure what to do."

Hailey pointed behind me, "I thought maybe he would know what to do."

I twisted around to see the 'him' she was talking about, slumped over in a chair, snoring loudly.

Julius.

"We both tried everything we could think of to wake you up. But you just wouldn't open your eyes. You kept calling out and your body kept shaking."

Rias squeezed harder for a moment and then relaxed her grip around me. Looking at her face was heartbreaking. Her bloodshot eyes swelled as tears fell down her face. I was able to rasp two words from my throat.

"I-I'm s-sorry..."

She took my face in her hands and leaned in close. Her forehead came to rest on mine.

Hailey crept up onto the bed laid down beside us, her head coming in to rest against Rias' and mine.

"I'm going to keep you safe."

Her words were calming. The tension in my body released and my eyes stung as my own tears swelled. I leaned into her, burying my head into her lap.

My words scratched against my throat as I spoke, "It was a Terror Demon, I think. It attacked me—" I looked down at myself, notably unharmed, "Well, not physically, it's more like it attacked my own thoughts..."

I told Hailey and Rias every detail of my nightmare. Afterwards, Hailey placed her hands on my shoulders.

"I think... I think that we don't tell anyone about this."

"I agree with Hailey."

Before I could respond, Hailey jumped off the bed and gave Julius' chair a kick. He jolted awake, startled, he reached for a sword that wasn't there. He looked from Hailey, to Rias, to me—and seeing I was awake, he relaxed.

"Finally up from your nap, your highness?" he snickered.

A nod is all I managed to give him as a response. From the battle and from sweating all night, I was dehydrated and weak.

Julius had already picked up on that, and handed me his water canteen. I started with a few small sips. The refreshing touch against my dry throat was more than my mind could handle, I threw moderation to the wind, and was gulping down the water in a moment.

"Here."

Julius startled me, his arm was outstretched towards me holding something. With a death-glare I turned towards him, but my expression softened as I saw what he was trying to thrust at my face.

Upon a small plate sat a little muffin-cake topped with fresh berries and—*was that cream!?*

"Take it. Happy birthday, or whatever."

I could read him like a book. Even though he wore a scowl on his face, I knew he was actually embarrassed about his awkward presentation of the cake.

"Thanks, Julius. I really appreciate it."

My lips were still dry, and the wide smile that took hold on my face was painful as the skin cracked.

I shared the cake with the three of them. The sweet cream and the sour berries gave the fluffy cake a bright taste that energized my mood.

Today was the twentieth of Capri'æni Ix. The month under the sign of Capricorn, ♑. It was my birth anniversary.

The only three people here who would know that were sitting next me—and after the short panic that we all experienced, birthday wishes were the furthest thing from our minds.

It was also the midpoint of the month. If you believed in the Celestial Faith, today would be the day where Capricorn's power and influence over this world was at its greatest. Back in Axio, there would be a festival and a night of drinking and dancing—well, there would have been. Probably not anymore.

Hailey managed to find a new uniform for me to wear, replacing the torn mess I had stripped off last night.

Rias gave me a tight squeeze after I had fastened the last of my uniform's straps. Her quiet voice lightened my mood a little, and I was ready for the day.

"Happy birthday big sister! Stay safe out there today, okay?"

Outside, the air was chilly and damp. Puddles of mud were the landscape of our campsite now. Ominous gray clouds threatened us overhead.

The mood was mixed. About half of the guardsmen were cheerful. They were recounting last night's battle, embellishing the number of enemies slain into the thousands. The other half looked like they were ready to break if someone looked at them wrong. Maybe the stress from battle was getting to them.

Or maybe it was something else... It's possible I wasn't the only one to suffer a nightmare last night.

We ran into Luke and Hanna at the field kitchen, they were leaving and gave us a warning. The ration this morning was over-salted hardtack and questionable looking 'meat'.

Leftover field marmot...

We found a table and I poked at my meal while absentmindedly surveying the room. The same mixed-emotions were obvious here as well. Some tables were full of laughter. Others looked like ours, with their occupants sitting silently and barely eating.

Hailey nudged me, bringing my attention back to our table.

"Let's check in with Dori after this. Hopefully she was able to take a look at your shoulderplates."

"Yeah, good idea." I ran my hands over my shoulders. "Feels like I'm walking around with myself exposed without them."

Julius choked on a bite of his biscuit.

Hailey goaded him, "Were you just imaging our Commander exposed, Julius?"

"Ye' really took ah' beatin' last night, didnae' ya'?"

"You should see the other guy."

Dori was tapping a ball-ended hammer against a piece of red painted metal. Laid out on the table nearby were other assorted pieces of my armor.

"Saw th' massive club them Divisionals had hauled 'ere last nigh'. Thought to meself, 'Dinnae this look like an absolute shite-fest'."

She handed me the plate she was hammering. It was one of my shoulderplates, rounded back into shape.

"Replaced th' paddin' on those too. Should feel like new on 'yer shoulders."

"Thank you, Dori. I really appreciate it."

She grabbed a small crate from another table and placed it in front of me. Peeking inside, I could see parts of Julius' armor.

I returned to the mess hall and dropped the crate down behind Julius. He whipped his head back, startled. Glancing up to me, down to the crate, to where I was sitting before, and then back to me.

Rias smiled back at us from my previous spot.

"By the Celestials I didn't even know you left." He looked back at Rias, "You look exactly like your sister. It's uncanny."

We headed to the command tent and ran into Soren and Alistaire. They were sitting on a makeshift bench, a long timber that had been sawed down to create a flat surface and sunken into the ground. Soren's head bobbed down a few times, popping back up to catch himself from drifting back to sleep. Alistaire was leaning against him, eyes closed and a small sliver of drool was seeping down his chin.

Soren's head popped up from a downward bob and his body twitched, nudging his sleeping companion awake.

Alistaire sat up and wiped his arm across his mouth. As he turned he caught sight of us approaching.

"Oh! Uhm, morning all."

"Hey Alistaire. Hey Soren. You two been waiting long?"

"Not too long. We've been up for a while though. Hard to sleep when your whole body is sore."

"I don't think any of us got any rest either." I pointed to Hailey, Julius, and myself. "Speaking of rest, have you seen the rest of the party? We ran into Luke and Hanna earlier, but I haven't seen Mei all morning."

They both shifted uneasily on the bench. Soren's eyes darted away from my gaze.

"So I take that as a yes. What kind of trouble did she get herself into?"

Alistaire opened his mouth briefly, as if to speak, but shut it quickly and pursed his lips.

Narrowing my eyes, I leaned in close to them.

"Boys, tell me where she is."

We found Mei in the midst of an argument at the armory. The Quartermaster was standing firm about the 'absurd' amount of arrows she was requesting.

Mei's position was that it was not absurd, and that she had run out of arrows last night. Proof enough that the quantity she requested was reasonable.

I intervened when things seemed like they were about to turn into a shouting match. Confronting the two of them, I asked how many arrows we were talking about.

Mei replied quickly, 'only' four-hundred.

I wasn't sure where she was going to pack away four-hundred arrows, but an annoyed 'Just give her what she asked for' from Julius and we were on our way to the stables.

Luke was already there bridling the horses.

Hanna briefed us that she had already dispatched eighteen other parties to Tolin in the early morning. These parties were organized into raiding teams of three, so each group would have about twenty people. They would be clearing and securing buildings one sector at a time.

Our party would be going in as a vanguard again, to clear a way through the garrison district.

A blood-soaked mess greeted us at the gates of Tolin. Large timbers with crude planks hammered into place had been laid into the mud to create a walkable pathway into the city. The demon corpses from last night had been removed. Great pyres had been erected in a newly dug pit some distance from the gatehouse. The smell of burning flesh stung my nose.

Entering the market square we were greeted by the commanding officer, a Knight-Lieutenant.

Their rundown was simple, the six raiding teams were deployed to the remaining three districts; Residential, Port, Garrison. There were two teams per district, and about forty members per team.

We were now supposed to link up with the Garrison team, who were assisting with clearing the riverside promenade of the residential district. Once together, we'd form up as a single raiding division.

A division at its smallest was a militarized group of two or more raid-sized parties led by an uppercore officer. At its largest, you had major divisions like Hailey's.

Before the coup, the Third Division was around one-hundred and fifty officers, and over two-thousand five-hundred divisionals. That single division is too large to handle on its own, so it's broken down further into more manageable divisions, such as the raiding team we were about to form.

The Garrison Citadel loomed over the residential district. The red-stone contrasted sharply with the walls, almost isolating it from the rest of the city.

The street leading to the Citadel was a wide unbending paved through-way. Most of the buildings lining the street were single-family homes, capable of housing no more than five or six adults. Branching from the main street were many winding arterial roads. These led off to all sorts of varying neighborhoods, some of the same single-family homes, some larger homes, and even a few manors.

"Hail Commanders, and good morning," A steel-clad Paladin saluted our approach, "We're clearing the last remaining block of residences. My teams should be back in about an hour."

Hailey had taken hold of my hand on our walk through the city and I fumbled momentarily trying to return the Paladin's salute. Hailey snickered at my clumsiness.

"Good timing. Will you be ready to move forward when they return?"

The Paladin motioned over her wrist and a rune glowed brightly. A large party interface danced in the mists.

"We'll be ready."

I waved over my own rune and brought up the party interface. I sent the Paladin a request to merge her party into ours. She accepted, and my view quickly grew to show an unmanageable amount of party members.

The two teams responsible for the residential district had joined under a single group with the two garrison teams. By accepting my merge request, I had added over one-hundred-sixty new members to my group.

I raised my eyebrow at the Paladin. She shrugged and gave me a look that said 'I'm just doing my job here, lady'.

The awkward exchange had garnered the attention of my six party members—they looked at me expectantly.

"Good news, we're the proud leaders of a small army." I joked, "It's us, plus four whole raiding teams."

Luke and Hailey both stared, slack jawed. First at the Paladin, then at me. I stared blankly back at them.

"I knew nothing about this."

Julius broke the brief tension.

"Last night, I asked Hanna to relay orders to consolidate the raiding teams when they got close to the Citadel. After our encounter last night... I wanted to play things safe."

"We've never fielded a singular force this large before, Julius."

"Well you know what they say, never a time like the present."

"I don't think that saying applies to commanding four raiding teams through a derelict castle."

"Difference of opinion I guess." He shrugged and flashed me a grin.

Bastard.

I spent the next hour reviewing my party configurations, trying to make mental notes to remember which members were defenders, casters, soldiers, or rangers.

Ultimately I resigned in defeat.

There were just way too many to make a meaningful effort. One-hundred-seventy-two members in total, including myself and my party. I counted twice to confirm the number.

There were twenty-three healer specialty casters between the four teams. Adding in Hailey, I wouldn't need to focus on watching anyone's life bars. She would let me know if they needed help.

The raid team members joined us at the square that was just before the garrison district's gatehouse.

The garrison gatehouse was noticeably different from any other in the city. Instead of the pinkish-white *Vyae* stone, it was constructed from rare, red granite. Practically all important structures from the old Vanixian Empire were built from this type of stone. It was incredibly tough from a hardness level, but it was near-impossible to penetrate with magick. The crystalline formation of the stone absorbed all types of magick and would become harder and more resilient the more spells that were cast upon them. Stonemason Guilds that built with this type of stone typically charged exorbitant rates that could empty the pockets of even the wealthiest nobles.

Also noticeable, was that the gate was suspiciously shut. All the other gates in the city had been locked in an open position, which was pretty standard for a city that was caught unaware during an attack. The fact that this gate was shut, implied it was closed some time after the city fell, or it was closed before or during the attack.

None of the scouting teams had breached the Citadel. We had no way of knowing if there were more hordes of demons nested here, or if it was abandoned.

That uncertainty obviously being the exact reason Julius arranged for four raiding teams to accompany us.

Luke and two other rogues made their way into the gatehouse to find the mechanism that would raise the inner gate. Their bodies shimmered and faded away in stealth.

Ten minutes passed and a loud 'click' was heard from above the gateways corridor. Another 'click' a minute after that, and the grinding and scraping of the gate raising gnawed at my ears.

Luke and his partners emerged from the gatehouse and waved us over.

"There are clear indications of recent movement in the halls leading up to gate controls."

"Great, squatters. Think they'll just leave if we ask nicely?"

Soren sighed at Alistaire's attempt at humor.

"Be ready for anything," I warned my party, "keep your guard up. Call out anything that seems out of place —"

A familiar scraping noise followed by dark runes appearing above the gate cut me off.

The flash of words etching in my mind stopped me in my tracks, "TURN BACK OR BE CONSUMED."

The deep recessed voice, the same as from my demonic nightmare, emanated from my own mind and sent sharp jolts of pain through my head.

I looked to Hailey, but her expression said it all. She heard the voice as well.

Almost every member of the raid had the same pained look on their face. A look of shock and panic paired with a clenched jaw, fighting through the searing pain each word inflicted on them.

The only two people seemingly unaffected were Julius and Mei, though I'm sure he was just being stoic.

I would bet that he was screaming on the inside.

Mei's eyes were trained on the darkness beyond the gatehouse.

"Commander."

"Y-yeah, Mei?" I grimaced through the residual pain.

"Terror Demon."

"Terror Demon, or one of the Celestials themselves, it's in my castle."

Julius brought his shield off its mounting plate on his back and unsheathed his sword. Calmly he gave orders, "Mei, you're on point with me. Airis, you stay two lengths behind me. Soren. Alistaire. Take up positions on Airis. Luke, stick to Hailey like glue. Don't let anything get close to her."

Silver light glowed from Julius' shield as he spoke an incantation, "Light, grant us Strength. For in Strength we find Power. In Power we create Unity. In Unity, we serve the righteous and bring forth justice to these tainted lands. Despair forces of darkness, Silver Bulwark!"

The raid was enveloped in its glow. The protective barrier would provide a great defense boost to everyone.

Channeling my own power, I began to cast my own aura.

"Source of light that dwells among the veiled. Journey with us as we make our way in the darkness. Come forth and guide our way, Radiance!"

The soft golden glow swept over the raid. I turned to face my small army, to offer them some sort of encouraging words...

I don't know what to say at a moment like this...

In an effort to avoid embarrassing myself at this critical point, I drew my blade and raised it above my head. It sparked to life, the rush of crimson flame roared over me.

A war cry echoed through the stone gateway into the halls of the Citadel. Four words in defiance of the usurper hiding inside.

"For the Crimson Blade!"

NINE

THE CITADEL HALLS WERE THICK WITH Aethermist. The twisting corridors were a maze on their own, but with the mist it was labyrinthine.

Shadows danced in the mist, playing tricks on our eyes. They caused some junior members to lose their composure—occasionally the sound of an arrow hitting a wall or a spell fizzling out on the stone, followed by an expletive was heard behind us.

We were now slowly making our way through a massive central antechamber. Numerous pathways branched off but we advanced straight through into the largest archway. The chamber opened up into a grand hall. Intricate stained glass windows lined both walls. Though most of them were severely damaged and even shattered, a few managed to have survived relatively in one piece. They depicted powerful warriors, clad in ornamental armor and wearing the crest of the Vanixian Empire, a great Phoenix with its wings spread wide.

Large fluted pillars of granite rose up through the hall, each one disappearing into a seemingly endless void. From this darkness hung large chains, some swaying freely and others held taut by wrought iron chandeliers.

As the last member stepped into the hall, runes formed ahead of us. Magickal energy crackled around them, but no mental assault followed.

A bolt of purple magick shot overhead, striking the archway. A barrier formed in the threshold.

An elemental seal.

The seal flashed brightly, and three runes formed in front of it.

That spiteful voice hammered in my head this time, "NO RETREAT COME FACE DEATH."

There was certainly no retreat. The seal that prevented our escape was Void Magick, and there were few among the mortal races that could channel that power. We would have to defeat the Terror Demon if we wanted to escape this nightmare.

Mei signaled for the group to stop and everyone came to a halt. The clank of steel subsided and an eerie silence fell over us.

But not for long.

The sound of something creaking in the mists broke the silence. The noise grew louder and started emanating from all across the hall. Out of the mists shapes started to appear.

Skeletal warriors shambled towards us. They wore ornamental red armor, and their equipment was a mix of heavily armored knights to light armed rangers.

This demon literally wants us to face Death.

I scanned the closest skeleton warrior.

TARGET	STATISTICS	VALUES
RISEN DEAD	HEALTH	50 / 50
	STAMINA	50 / 50
	MAGICKA	0 / 0

These were some incredibly weak foes.

In a one-on-one fight, any soldier could easily win. However, this was not a dueling tournament. We were outnumbered and the number of enemies was growing at an alarming rate as more of the undead poured in from the mists.

Julius cried out orders and defensive positions started to form.

Guardians formed compact shieldwall formations around our larger force. The clash of steel against bone and sinew echoed through the halls.

Rangers formed a firing line towards the back and unleashed a volley. Arrows rained down on the approaching horde of undead, but they did little to stagger their advance. Most failed to hit a mark or they simply glanced off the bones, failing to find any substance to stick their bladed heads into. Julius was quick to organize the rangers into a melee position after the failed volley.

Bursts of elemental fury sailed overhead as casters slung their spells at the enemy. Balls of fire and lightning struck their targets and exploded in an area of effect that devastated the oncoming horde.

For every undead fiend slain, another flooded in from the dark abyss surrounding us.

A group of rangers flanked me on my right. They each wielded short-bladed swords called FAELX CRESAERIE in elvish, or commonly referred to as crescent glaives by Divisionals. These swords were subtly curved with a single-edged blade. Typically held backwards against the wielder's forearm, their short nature and aerodynamic blade allowed for their users to twist and dance around the battlefield, slashing their enemies apart in fluid motion.

One of the members stuck out, her eyes met mine from under a cowled hood. It was Mei. No longer on point, she must have fallen back with the rest of the rangers after the battle started.

"We need to push forward or we will be overrun."

Her words were sharp, without emotion as always.

She knew what I knew as well; that if we didn't gain ground and eliminate the source behind this foul void magick, our stamina would slowly be chipped away. Eventually our defensive lines would falter. After that, our forces would be routed—and with no way of escape...

We would all face death.

Poetic.

A group of undead broke through the shield line ahead of us and charged our position.

Overhead, Valiance, our ebonfeathered overwatch, cried sharply. The reddened glow of MARK TARGET illuminated the shambling bones. Crimson flames and crescent glaives danced through the air and the vanguard of the faceless dead crumbled to dust.

In a huff of fatigue I gave Mei a quick response.

"We'll push forward."

Committing to moving ahead, I activated the Communirune and reached out to the frontlines, focusing on Julius.

"Hey. Time to gain ground. Have any plans?"

"Just one, avoid dying."

"Great plan, really. Anything else you wanna add to that or—?"

"Nope."

The master strategist. Just yesterday Luke lavished praise worthy of a storybook hero. 'He's something else' Luke had said
—

BOOM!

A deafening explosion resonated from the frontline. It was followed by cries of pain, and some strong language in a gruff voice. I shot a frantic thought out to Julius.

"What happened, are you okay!?"

"..."

After a brief delay, and a few skipped heartbeats, he replied with a broken tone.

"One of those damned things just exploded. We lost three."

"Celestials..."

"I don't think they're gonna help us on this one, Airis. If you can rally troops and carve a path, do it. I'll do what I can to keep our forces moving forward with you."

I turned to Mei and gave her a sharp nod, "We're up."

I sprinted forward and pushed past the guardian's shieldwall. Mei and the other rangers followed close behind me—they struck with precision, quick slashes that tore cleanly through ligament and sinew.

My attacks were much more chaotic in contrast. Striking out in wide arcs, I cleaved throngs of the dead with each swing. Flames lashed out, carving a pathway for us to advance.

As we pushed forward, the remainder of our forces fell in behind us. It was not a strong defensive line, every inch of ground we gained was traded tit for tat with injury.

By the time we had crossed the length of the hall, twenty members in total were severely injured; another fifteen were dead.

The hall ended at a great imperial staircase. Red granite was inlaid within white marble to create a dazzling crosshatch pattern as the stairs rose up. Two divided flights arched away from a central landing, adorned with gold embellishment.

Our forces pushed onto the landing and the remaining guardians formed a shieldwall between the banisters on the base of the stairs. Rangers and casters took positions on the divided flights.

The onslaught of undead had slowed—or at least it appeared that way. Without the need to defend multiple flanks our forces could focus fire, and we took advantage of this to see to our wounded.

The injured soldiers were centered along the back wall of the landing. I scanned the Healer members of the raiding group, and was shocked to see that every one of them had almost depleted their magicka. Despite that, the Healers were already channeling spells to stop blood loss and heal wounds.

I spotted Hailey among them. She was examining a lightly armored woman, whose leg was twisted in a gruesome manner. As I got closer I could tell how bad the injury truly was. It was impossible to tell if there was a single definitive point the bleeding was coming from. Hailey's healing magic wasn't meant for damage like this. Spending high amounts of magicka to heal complicated wounds like this would leave her with a massive headache—and unable to function.

Nevermind the fact that she was almost completely out of magicka herself.

I placed a hand on her shoulder, "I've got this."

She spun around at my touch. Her eyes lit up when she realized it was me and mouthed a 'Thank you' at me. She looked like she was about to collapse any minute.

The bone needed to be set before I could cast my healing spell, otherwise the wound may heal up but the leg may not function properly. The woman was barely conscious. Explaining the process from setting to healing, I got a few nods from her and a raspy response through a clenched jaw.

"Just do what you have to..."

I channeled golden light through my palms.

"Blessed and divine light, I pray to you. Bestow your warmth unto me and save this one from harm. Heal!"

An hour had passed before our remaining force was back on their feet. Our defenses held against the horde of undead much easier with a single front. Cycling a few people at a time gave everyone a chance to catch their breath. Using what little supply we had brought with us, the casters had recovered a good portion of their magicka.

We were ready to push forward, but with swarms of undead tailing behind us the whole way there was no guarantee the path forward wasn't a death sentence that we were being herded to.

The way above the staircase led to a wide hallway with paths that branched off behind us in two walkways that encompassed the entire Grand Hall.

I was standing at the apex of the staircase looking down at the seemingly endless struggle against the undead when Julius came into view, brandishing his shield as if he were about to lead a charge forward into the sea of death—Instead, the shield started to glow with a soft silver light. The light's intensity grew and others took notice of his weird stance.

Blinding silver light erupted from his shield. A deafening ringing of metal chains clashing against each other filled my ears. A silver wall had formed between our guardians and the mass of undead soldiers.

Metal chains had been interwoven to create—what was in simplest terms—a net.

A heavily armored skeletal warrior charged the net, but was blasted backwards in a bright flash of light. More of the undead charged against the netting, enraged by the previous blast. They met the same fate.

"That should hold for an hour. At the most. Time to move forward." Julius, the now center of attention, walked up the stairway and the raid members followed.

The main hallway was constructed and decorated in a similar fashion as the hall we were leaving but with one distinct difference—

"Celestials above..." My heart sank at the unnerving sight.

There were hundreds of human skulls piled up from the floor reaching up the arches and pillars. Gasps of shock continued down the formation as the main force rounded the stairs. An eerie silence fell over the raid. I looked to my companions for comfort, but was met with looks of unease and worry.

"Groups One and Three, take center and form a forward line. Group Two, stay in the rear and keep that shieldwall tight. Group Four, fall in with the main force." Julius' orders clipped sharply in the hushed hallway. Words that should have echoed against the stone walls were dulled by the collection of grim totems that lined them.

The muffled footsteps of armored soldiers moving into positions disturbed the silence. The forward group formed up at the entrance to the hallway. The rest of us fell in behind them a few paces back.

"Move out!"

More skulls lined a massive doorway. Enormous wooden doors hung squarely in place, reinforced by steel plating. This was the entrance to the Grand Hall's Commander's Quarters.

Beyond these doors would have housed a lavish bedroom complete with a meeting room, a bath, and a small kitchen.

The guardians in the front pushed the doors in. They creaked open and slammed hard against the stone walls. Instead of a regal room fit for a noble, we met a grotesque display. The soft white stones in the floor were stained red and covered in dried blood. Along the walls on large metal pikes—human remains hung, impaled through the chest.

Julius took point while I followed closely behind with my sword ready. The dried blood cracked like mud beneath our footsteps. A feeling of dread came over me and a shiver ran down my spine.

The last member of the raid crossed into the room. I expected the doorway to shut and seal with another void seal, but nothing happened.

Julius continued to creep towards the center of the room. His shield shined brightly, a beacon of hope in contrast to the unease this gore filled room emitted. That bulwark was his only piece of equipment that didn't look like it had been damaged in a magickal blast. There were dents, punctures, and bends in the metal plating of his armor.

Soren and Alistaire followed closely behind him. Their equipment didn't look any better than Julius'. Soren's steps were hobbled, an uneven stride that favored his right side.

I brought up my party interface. Next to Soren's interface was a small icon. Focusing on it, I was confronted with a grim message.

» SOREN SUFFERS FROM A CRIPPLED LEG

Hailey had come up to me and leaned her head against my back. I gasped when I read the message, my gaze lingered on Soren.

"He took a blow from a warhammer. Shattered his knee completely."

"What the—why would anyone heal it like that!?"

I was incredulous—I was so angry!

I was worried for my friend.

"He had passed out from shock and blood loss... Alistaire dragged him to a healer. It was either that, or he'd die."

"..."

I looked towards Alistaire. He was cautiously scanning the room, but he did glance over at Soren every few seconds.

"Sigils!"

I whipped my head to look for who had called out. An armored figure was pointing up towards the ceiling. Two sigils were forming above us.

"SO YOU HAVE CHOSEN DEATH."

Painful reverberations that felt like they could fracture my skull trembled through my head. The voice was louder than before. Each word felt like a hammer blow to my psyche.

The others in the raid had the same reaction as me. Some were doubled over in pain, cradling their heads between both hands. Others had fallen to their knees and cried out.

Soren and Alistaire leaned against each other, clutching arms.

Even the stoic Silver Bulwark himself had dropped down, leaning against his shield anchored in the paved floor.

Three more sigils appeared in place of the first two.

The fracturing voice hammered again, "THEN YOU WILL DIE."

A thick dark mist flooded into the chamber causing visibility to fall drastically. I could see clearly about an arm's length in front of me, but past that things started to become blurred and shadowed.

The flames of my sword did little to abate the encroaching darkness—though they did illuminate the mists around me. Effectively turning me into a beacon of light.

Hailey stumbled through the mist a few paces, and was now clutching the loose fabric of my sleeve.

"I–I really don't like this..."

I didn't like this either. I was terrified. I wasn't sure I'd even be able to mutter a single word of comfort to her.

They say your life flashes through your mind before you die.

Though I wasn't yet dead—images of dead friends and comrades flooded mine. Towers of stone crumbling down around us. Hungry flames licking at our back as we fled home.

A frustrated scream, pleading for Julius to leave me behind and go with the rest of our people... to let me stay behind and sacrifice myself.

I clenched my right hand into a fist and lifted my sword with my left.

"We have to kill this demon. We conquer this city or die trying. There is no other outcome that is acceptable, and we have no other option."

A terrible shriek pierced the mists. My attention turned to where the awful noise had come from.

Three figures could be made out in front of us. A silver shield held high in the air. A wave of energy washed over us as Julius activated his SILVER BULWARK ability.

The mists stirred around them—swirling as if something was circling them. A dark mass came between us and broke my sight line.

The mass rose up out of the mists. Bowed legs that bent backwards as the figure stood, towered over us. Thick muscles rippled across its skin. Its head turned slowly, and where you'd expect eyes—glowing purple flames flickered in their place. The creature's head looked like that of a hammershark, something that you'd find in the deep ocean.

Infinite rows of jagged fangs smiled a wicked grin at me.

It was the creature from my nightmare.

This was the Terror Demon.

The true battle over the garrison was about to begin.

And with a movement so fast that I couldn't see that the monster had even moved, a long arm crashed down on the three shadowy figures huddled in the mists.

"Aaaah–"

"S-Soren!"

A blood curdling scream echoed through the halls...

TEN

AS QUICK AS THE FIRST ATTACK THE TERROR Demon struck again in a wild second assault. Its other arm came down with blinding speed, but was blocked in a shower of sparks as Julius' shield came up to meet it.

The force of the impact sent Julius flying backwards, tumbling into Alistaire. The two of them faded from view into the mist...

"Guardians to the front, secure our flanks! Dodge its attacks, do not try to block. Rangers, fire at will!—cripple its arms if you can!"

The words escaped my mouth without registering what I was saying. Pure fury had taken over my senses and I was shouting orders.

"Hit that demon with everything you've got!"

I still had my party interface up when Soren took the initial blow. I had watched in disbelief as his health plummeted into the black.

My soldiers rushed forward, despite the grim fate of the three men who had been ahead of them. Arrows rained down on the gargantuan demon. The broadheads ripped into its flesh, damaging muscle and tendon.

The quick succession of the barrage caused the demon to stumble briefly, giving an opening to the charging soldiers.

"Airis...?"

Hailey's voice was meek. I glanced at her, and saw that she also had a party interface in view. Her eyes were locked to the three darkened lines that listed the names of our friends.

"We can't do anything about that right now."

"..."

I couldn't leave her here in this state—but time was not on our side. Every moment that passed could be another soldier's death. The guardians engaging the demon were doing well holding the aggression while casters and rangers rained down fire from afar. I had a little time to get her back into the fight.

There had to be a way to snap her out of the shock. I took her hand and lifted her head. Her eyes trembled as tears cascaded down her cheeks. My chest tightened.

"...Hails, I need you to focus."

"I don't want to lose you!" She blurted out in response.

Her confession left me weak in the knees. I was flushed, and had to try hard to keep my own emotions in check.

"It might feel like it," I brushed away a stream of tears from her cheek, "but it wouldn't be the end of the world. We all die, sooner or later. It's just a facet of life."

"I know—"

"There are worse things."

"... I know."

"And we don't have a choice."

"It just frightens me so much. How can you act so calm?"

I pressed my forehead against hers and squeezed her hands. We stood there silently for a few seconds before I gave her a final squeeze and pulled back.

"Because this is my consequence. I wanted to save our people, and that decision brought us here. I made my choice... and you made yours to follow me, that's all there is to it. I don't think we chose wrong."

She was silent, but it looked like her mood had improved.

"Watch my back, okay?"

She nodded and while wiping away her tears, she steadied herself against the dread, "Okay."

I turned to the behemoth in the center of the hall and swiped over on my interface.

Time to see what we're up against.

TARGET	STATISTICS	VALUES
ASTERYITH ARCHDEMON	HEALTH	24213 / 25000
	STAMINA	752 / 800
	MAGICKA	2560 / 2800

My mouth was open wide in disbelief. The stat points of this monster were incredible. I looked back at Hailey, just to check that she was still with me. She was—though not so resolute as she was moments ago.

"Well, this could take a while." I nervously chuckled and readied my blade for combat.

"Aaarrgghh"

I growled in frustration as my WILD STRIKE was swatted away by Asteryith's heavy arm.

"—channel the goodwill of your power and deliver them from harm. Healing Grace!"

Hailey's voice wavered loudly nearby as golden light washed over me, the sharp pain from the last parried attack soothed to a dull ache.

She had been casting a healing spell after almost every attack, just to keep me from getting injured. Even a simple parry would drop nearly half of my health.

This monster's power was like nothing we had ever faced. Nothing in the Academy could have trained us for this.

A streak of green blitzed past my right side, impacting the Archdemon's left shoulder just as it was raising its arm to strike. I glanced back to see Mei powering up another shot.

Her timed shots were interrupting the heavier attacks; after that first two-hit combo... She had been doing her best to protect our front liners.

Beside her, Luke's shadowy figure danced in the shadows. A glint of metal blinked and a small knife soared through the air.

It struck a small crease in the demon's back-bent knees, causing the monster to flinch ever so slightly. The simple trick did little damage to the beast as a whole, but the delay in movement allowed a small group of exhausted warriors to fall back.

His voice called out to the retreating unit,

"Group Three switch out with Four! Two, you're next in rotation."

More runes appeared above Luke's location. They wavered in the air, seemingly fading in and out.

"YOUR EFFORTS ARE FOOLISH."

The booming voice struck from inside my head as usual, but this time it was noticeably less debilitating.

"Flames that burn beyond the veil, gather by my will, Fireball!"

A fiery blast from a Divisional Mage hit Asteryith near the neck. The explosive energy enveloped its face in a swirl of flames and smoke.

I leapt forward and swung with all the strength I could muster. My blade made contact with its left arm and BLADE SLASH dug deep into the flesh.

I prayed for a critical strike.

If I could get a critical hit, SOULFIRE might just overwhelm the Archdemon.

Flames raced over its pale skin, dealing burning damage in a wide area of effect as they etched deeply—but no critical effect.

Two runic sigils flashed in front of me, fading away quickly.

"I CANNOT BE STOPPED."

A deep throaty roar shook the room as Asteryith wailed. The sound was drastically different than the rumbling voice that spoke inside our minds. The roar from the demon felt more primeval. The sound of a terrifying beast from the dawn of creation.

Asteryith swung its arm down towards me—another bolt of green struck hard against its shoulder. Expecting the attack to be interrupted, I was taken by surprise when its giant clawed hand continued to bear down on me. I rolled out of the way, barely avoiding the hit.

Dark violet energy rippled across the demon's skin down to its claws.

"Get back, evade!—"

My order didn't come fast enough...

The demon spun in a vicious whirlwind attack. The strike sent the seven soldiers of Group Three flying back into the air. They fell in a crash of steel onto the stone below, lying motionless.

"Celestials..."

Its wild spinning left the demon stopped within an arm's reach of Mei. Luke burst forth from his stealthed position to launch a surprise attack.

His short blade trailed behind him in a faint green light. He thrust the sword in two horizontal slashes, and blades of light rushed forward ahead of him. Luke jumped up and brought his sword down in a final swing that intersected the light, striking at the apex of the monster's chest.

The downward swing cut cleanly through the tough hide of the demon. Both blades of light flared as Luke's sword passed through them, expanding outwards and burning the demon's exposed tissue, causing a roar in response.

Asteryith raised its arm in a quick jerk motion to counterattack, striking one of the large stone pillars as it clawed downwards at Luke. The impact with the pillar knocked the attack off course, allowing Luke to disengage to safety.

In a rage, the beast's other arm swiped in from the right, aimed directly for Luke. He raised an arm to block, but ducked down at the last moment, attempting a feint.

"Shadows protect me, Evasion!"

His body twisted away, leaving behind only a small silver runic sigil traced in the air. He gracefully missed the razor sharp claws—but when the fist impacted the floor beneath him, Luke lost his footing. He fell backwards on a twisted leg.

The loud pop and painful cry indicated a worst possible outcome. I confirmed in my party interface, Luke was suffering from an impairment effect.

Asteryith lifted both arms high into the air with a giant leap. Its towering body impacted the pillar once more, causing a large chunk to break loose. The rounded stone crashed down like a felled redwood tree. A deep groan filled the air as the aging roof buckled under the lost support.

Stone arches and wooden beams rained down above Luke and Mei's position. Mei rolled and dodged the falling debris with elvish grace—but Luke was not so agile. He was limping with an injured ankle in my direction with a small group of soldiers who had rushed in to grab him.

An earsplitting snap overhead was followed by a large timber beam crashing down just behind them. Ceramic roof tiles fluttered down, fracturing on impact and turning the scene into a fragmentation hazard.

One of the soldiers supporting Luke yelped as sharp splinters of hardened clay pierced her back. They almost faltered, but managed to recover from a stumble that would've left them all in a danger zone.

Bright sunlight filled the hall, illuminating the hellscape of gore and sadism. Asteryith roared in rage once more as another beam fell squarely on top of the beast. The blow knocked it forwards into the sun. A high-pitched wail rose up from the demon as it reacted to the light.

It lept backwards to avoid the bright beam filling the room, leaving a substantial distance between my raid party and itself.

I frantically searched for Mei as the debris rain cleared. Checking her name on my interface showed she had lost a great deal of health, but she was still with us somewhere. I focused on her and called out through runic magick.

"Mei! Are you okay?"

No response.

"Mei! If you can hear me please say something!"

The empty silence stung my ears.

I prayed to the Celestials to steel me against the dread and unease that washed over me. My disarrayed soldiers needed a rallying cry. This was our chance for a last push to take down this cursed creature.

A quick scan gave me hope that it might now be on its last stand.

TARGET	STATISTICS	VALUES
ASTERYITH ARCHDEMON	HEALTH	1852 / 25000
	STAMINA	237 / 800
	MAGICKA	2750 / 2800

I frantically searched my mind for the right thing to say. Whatever I said could be my last words. I glanced at Hailey, who was already looking at me. Her presence calmed my racing heart.

The soldiers had gathered around us, looking to the both of us expectantly. My voice was hoarse and my hands shook nervously, but I steeled myself.

"I won't let our history fade away like we were never here, I refuse to be forgotten! Soldiers of the Republic, rise up and hear your Empress! You are the true descendants of a great Empire. This is the Land of the Light, this monster of darkness cannot be allowed to defile our homeland. We are reborn in the flames of the Vanixian Phoenix. I do not fear Death!"

I thrust my sword into the air, its dark crimson flames surged violently. Hailey came to stand behind me and raised up her staff to meet my blade. The fiery ethereal wings flared brightly, amplified in the light of the sun.

"We are the children of the Light! We defend against the dark abyss because it is our duty! For the Empire, for our Empress, for the Crimson Blade!

Her soft and girlish voice had been stowed away, in its place a stoic tone had risen up. Golden light spilled out of the oval gem-egg atop her staff.

"Shining light, shield us in all directions! In hands divine, embolden our life, Fortitude!"

Her final words, crescendoed loudly, echoing against the stones. The golden light spilled out over every member of the raid.

» YOU ARE AFFECTED BY FORTITUDE

In response the haggard remnants shouted back,
"For the Empire!"
"Fight for the Crimson Blade!"
Steel clashed against steel as the three remaining guardians slapped their swords against their shields in a rhythmic drumming.

BANG. BANG. BANG.

Soldiers formed up behind them in a long V formation.

"Push this darkspawn into the light, let it face the judgment of a mighty Empire. Forward into battle! Charge!"

I let out a primal yell and sprinted through the light to meet our foe. The demon screeched a deafening cry in response, shaking the foundation of the castle.

My blade sliced across its legs, forcing it to jump back in defense. As it found its footing, the entire arsenal of our raid came down upon it. Spears struck from behind as swords slashed at its sides.

The gauntlet of weaponry forced it to face me, or risk an attack of opportunity from my fiery blade if it tried to retaliate against my soldiers.

Asteryith's body lowered, and lunged forwards towards me in a wild charge.

I stepped back just in time to avoid a long arm rip past me. The rush of air nearly knocked me off balance. I brought my sword up quickly, anticipating the other arm which slashed at me a moment later.

Swinging the blade outwards I made contact with the demon's claws, parrying the attack by deflecting the massive hand away.

The demon jumped back before I could counter with a riposting BLADE SLASH.

Dark purple flames leered at me from across the hall. The looming figure heaved in the shadowy mists.

Its stamina must be reaching a critical point.

A high pitched screech cried out from the demon, but I maintained my composure.

No way I'm letting you get the better of me with some cheap tricks.

Asteryith dipped downwards to ready itself for another charge. In a blur, its legs kicked back and jagged claws bore down on me.

I held my blade out in front to brace for impact.

Gripping the long handle with my left hand, and pushing my right palm against the blade, I readied myself for the attack.

The demon's large body slammed into me with terrifying force.

My heels slid back against the blood encrusted stones.

I leaned into my sword, desperate to stay on my feet. I had been pushed a few feet back into the light, now a fair distance from the demon's reach. It turned away from me, towards one of the flanking groups. I couldn't let the beast harm my people.

I won't let this bastard go! I'll stop you right here.

No more of my soldiers would die to the foul monster.

I lunged forward at the Archdemon, quickly closing the gap between us—but it was ready for me—I had misjudged its attack.

This was a trick... And I fell for it in my blood rage.

A whirlwind of claws slashed through the room, striking me in the side. I was lifted off the ground. The air in my lungs rushed out and a hot sensation spread through my chest.

My body stopped rising abruptly, as the attack's momentum reached its peak.

I craned my head down. A large claw was protruding from my abdomen. The scythe-like appendage had caused immense damage to my breastplate, cracking the metal plate from the impact.

Unable to gasp for breath, my chest spasmed. I tasted the sourness of blood in the back of my throat.

Shit.

The Archdemon flung its arm out, and I slid free from impalement. My body ragdolled across the floor. I tumbled over loose stones, finally coming to rest just under a pillar bordering the entryway to the hall.

I tried to lift an arm to push myself over, but shock was starting to set in and my body betrayed me. My muscles were set ablaze in pain.

"No!—Airis!"

Hailey's voice cracked as she cried out.

The sound of metal clapping hard against stone echoed in my ears as she sprinted towards me.

My body jostled as she lifted me to rest on her lap. Her arm cradled my head against her chest. A stream of tears flooded down her face onto my cheeks.

Sobs shook her body violently.

"N-No, no, no! You have to stay with me. Keep your eyes open, please!"

Her free hand was already building up a tremendous amount of energy around it. She began to cast a healing spell, taking the extra time to use one of its more complex incantations.

"Blessed and divine light, lend me your strength. Through me, channel the goodwill of your power, envelop me in the golden flame and deliver them from harm. Healing Grace!"'"

The intensity of the golden aura that followed was enough to blind someone if they looked directly at it. Powerful golden waves of healing magick flowed through me.

"The bleeding is stopping. You'll be okay. You're going to be okay. You have to be okay."

I groaned weakly as the excruciating pain abated.

I tried to tell her that I was going to be okay, that she shouldn't worry—but no words escaped my open mouth.

Hailey gently brushed a hand across my cheek. Her voice trembled as she spoke.

"Don't try to talk, just rest. Everything is going to be okay." A choppy sigh escaped from her. "I'm terrified of ending up alone... I-I don't know what I'll do if I lose you. So you have to stay with me."

She brushed the hair away from my face.

Unsteady and out of focus, I could see her panicked expression. The corners of her lips twitched as she fought back the urge to break down.

My adrenaline was crashing, lightheaded-ness was setting in quickly.

With my every effort I tried to speak, but my voice failed me once more. All I could do was gasp weakly at her. My hand reached up and caressed her face.

My strength gave out, the blood loss had taken its final toll. I watched the monsters' final points of health drain out on the mist projection. The light flickered as the display reached the black, and the projection faded away.

A piercing screech reached my ears, the final defiant cry of the Archdemon, Asteryrith. At the very least, I would take solace in knowing that the demon met its end in these final moments. In death, its hold over this city was shattered.

My people would be safe here. Hailey would lead them. Out of the ashes of a shattered empire, my prayer was for them to be born anew, like the symbol of my family's empire.

Rise up, my phoenixes.

My eyes closed and I was enveloped in an impenetrable blackness. My body drifted away, and with it: time stopped...

[to be continued]

AFTERWORD

Hello! This is Aeyla Reed, the author of The Rise of Chaos: Genesis.

I hope you enjoyed this first stage of Airis' journey. A lot happened in a short amount of time leaving a few unresolved and unanswered questions.

The world of Terae is at times brutal and unforgiving. I look forward to sharing the rest of this story with you in future volumes.

If this was your first time reading a novel in the 'LitRPG' fashion I trust some of the story devices seemed foreign. A world with crazy magick that allows its denizens to visualize their own strengths and watch them grow as they forge their own way. That was the original idea behind this story, and the 'LitRPG' genre elements were wonderful way for me to express that.

I've grown up with RPGs: tabletops, video games, and their literary counterparts. One thing that always stuck out to me with the novels written off those media always deviated away from the game elements that made them so much fun in the first place.

Leveling up. Learning new skills and spells. Getting that great upgrade to a piece of gear. These are the exciting parts about growing with a character. I wanted to create a story that kept that excitement along with its journey.

I also enjoy reading light novels. Whether they're translated Japanese light novels, or if they're original English light novels (OELN). Being able to pick up a story and read it in a sitting rather than working through thirty huge chapters over the course of two weeks appeals to my attention span, as well as my schedule.

A tremendous "THANK YOU!" to both my illustrator, rean_kidd, whom I bombarded the request of doing all these illustrations for this novel only a few months before its planned launch date, and Natalie, who gave me her unadulterated opinions, suggestions, and new ideas to my story and was never afraid to eviscerate a section.

Thank you to my friends and family who endured my constant outbursts of excitement every time I got a new illustration back, finished a chapter, and through every frustrating stage of self-publishing.

And most of all, an enormous thank you, reader, for taking an interest in my book!

I hope to see you all in the next volume.

Aeyla Reed